"THE LOST CONTINENT OF ATLANTIS MAY BE A MYTH"

said Dick Benson, "but that doesn't matter right now. There's a scientist missing who's very important to America's future, and we know he's a student of everything connected with Atlantis. And the man who collapsed on Fifth Avenue was holding tight to a medallion that pertains to Atlantis. Then, when the scientist's daughter, who has come to us for help, rushes away when she sees the newspaper article about the mysterious man with the medallion, there are too many coincidences!"

Dick Benson made two brief phone calls, then turned to confront his friends with this startling announcement, "According to both the hospital and the FBI, the newspaper story is a hoax. There is no such person as THE MAN FROM ATLANTIS."

Books In This Series

By Kenneth Robeson

Published By

WARNER PAPERBACK LIBRARY

the Avenger

THE MAN FROM ATLANTIS

by Kenneth Robeson

WARNER
PAPERBACK
LIBRARY

A Warner Communications Company

WARNER PAPERBACK LIBRARY EDITION
First Printing: June, 1974

This Warner Paperback Library Edition is published
by arrangement with The Condé Nast Publications Inc.

Cover illustration by George Gross

Warner Paperback Library is a division of Warner Books, Inc.,
75 Rockefeller Plaza, New York, N.Y. 10019.

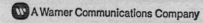 A Warner Communications Company

Printed in the United States of America

THE MAN
FROM ATLANTIS

CHAPTER I

All Hallows Eve

Nobody paid any attention to him, even though he was bright green.

He came walking, somewhat unsteadily, across the dimmed Grand Central station. He put one bright green hand to his perspiring forehead as he lurched up the marble steps leading out to Vanderbilt Avenue.

This attracted no attention either. By this time of night, nearly nine o'clock, a staggering man wasn't an unusual sight in the Forty-second Street area. And since this was Halloween, even a staggering green man didn't draw a second glance.

The green man was wearing an inexpensive gray suit. His dark overcoat was open, flapping as he swayed along the night sidewalk. "Millions of dollars," he muttered, "millions of dollars."

A chubby blond girl in a grass skirt was standing in front of the Biltmore Hotel when he went by. She was holding onto the arm of a freckled young man in the uniform of a Marine sergeant. His wasn't a costume, he was a real Marine on leave. "Hey, buddy, what do you hear from Mars?" he called at the green man.

"Atlantis," mumbled the green man.

"Okay, Atlantis then. How are all the little green men?"

The green man kept moving. His face was splotched with perspiration. He tottered on, heading for Fifth Avenue. He tugged his right hand out of his pocket. Clutched tight in his bright green fingers was a golden medallion, about the size of a silver dollar. "He can . . . he can tell us, I tell you . . . I'll . . . I'll . . . I'll take it too . . ." The words trailed off.

He hesitated for a moment after turning the corner of Fifth. He seemed to be studying the wartime street as though he'd never seen it before. "A thousand years," the green man said. "A thousand years . . ."

He took five steps east. He turned his head around, a puzzled expression mingling with the grimace of pain. The left side of him collapsed first. His left leg went slack, no longer supported him. He made a swaying genuflection on the pavement, his loose overcoat ballooning around him. His right leg gave way. The green man fell forward. His head smacked the cement and began to bleed.

Struggling, one hand still in his pocket, he tried to get up. The best he could do was roll over onto his back. His eyes drifted shut, his mouth dropped open. His right hand was free. It still held tight to the gold medallion.

This being New York City no one approached the fallen man. One hurrying middle-aged man actually stepped right over him. Five minutes after he'd collapsed on the sidewalk a silver poodle trotted up and sniffed at him.

"Bobby, don't be naughty!" A stick-thin old woman in a huge fur coat pulled the curious poodle away by its leash.

Five more minutes passed before a patrolman came along. He glanced at his wristwatch, remarking to himself, "Didn't expect one this early." He bent over the green man and prodded him in the side with his night stick. "Okay, friend, rise and shine."

The green man did not respond.

The uniformed cop gave him another poke, a bit harder than the one before. "Come on, friend, it'll be a lot easier if you can walk into the wagon on your own power."

Still the sprawled man did not move.

The patrolman said, "That's some makeup job you got there." Frowning, he knelt beside the green man. "Say, are you sick or something?"

He put his hand against the man's forehead and discovered two things. The man was burning up with fever and the bright green color was not due to makeup.

9

Cole Wilson was sitting with his back to the soda fountain, his elbows resting on the imitation marble top as he leaned back. "What I can't understand, Mac," he said, "is how such a man as yourself, a man of undisputed scientific genius, can make such a foul hot fudge sundae." He held a half-empty sundae glass in one hand, in the other a pulp magazine he'd filched from the nearby newsstand rack.

"Listen to me, you ox-like birkie," replied Fergus MacMurdie in his burred voice, "you're lucky I let you sit here at all, frightening off paying customers and chocolate thumbprints all over the magazines."

"I'm fairly certain I draw in more customers than I repel, Mac," said Cole. "And you've got to admit I'm a lot more attractive than that plaster dentist you've got stuck in the display window yonder." Cole Wilson was just under six feet tall and, despite Mac's criticism, he was a quite good-looking young man. Dark-haired, broad-shouldered and with a left-handed smile.

"I'm surre," said the lean Scot, "that if you was to stop in at headquarters, Dick Benson could find something more useful for you to do."

Cole had been scanning a page in the bright-covered pulp magazine. Allowing it to snap shut, he deposited it on the counter behind him. "Far fetched," he said. "You ought to try to provide your customers with the higher forms of literature, Mac."

On the other side of the fountain counter MacMurdie merely grunted.

"If you ripped out that wall there," Cole went on, "you could stock matched sets of Dickens, Balzac and—"

Outside the drugstore a girl had screamed.

Before the last note of the cry had faded Cole was in action. He set the sundae glass aside, not spilling a drop, and raced to the street outside. For all his pretense of laziness, Cole Wilson was really a man of action.

A half a block up from the storefront a slim redhaired girl was struggling with two husky men. A four-door sedan, motor running, was doubleparked directly opposite the struggle. Its back door hung open.

"Well, it doesn't take Philo Vance to figure what these lads are up to," said Cole as he ran swiftly to aid the girl.

The larger of the two men had only one eye. The other socket was empty, hollow. Even so, he was the one who spotted Cole first. He let go the redheaded girl's shoulders, spun to face the advancing young man.

"There's a shortage of men, not girls," grinned Cole. "Plenty of them to go around, old chum. So you needn't steal them off the streets."

"Oof," said the one-eyed man. He'd swung at Cole, missed, and taken a jab in the midriff. Before he could straighten up Cole delivered a chopping blow to the side of his head.

"I like your tie, though." Cole caught hold of it. "South Seas, palm trees, a real Gauguin

11

feeling." Using the gagging man's tie as a lever Cole spun him away.

"Oof," said the one-eyed man as he hit flat out against the brick wall of a building.

"Darn," said Cole. "In the movies they always go right on through." He sighed, grabbed hold of the second man.

"Smart guy," snarled this one. He was a better fighter than his one-eyed associate. On his second try he connected with Cole's chin.

"Oof, if I may quote your now unconscious partner." Shaking his head to clear it, Cole punched the man twice in the ribs.

"Look out," warned the girl, "two more!"

Cole was concentrating on his immediate opponent, but he heard the doors of the hovering sedan slam twice.

"Whoosh!" exclaimed MacMurdie from somewhere in the immediate vicinity. "Two skurlies he can handle by himself, but if it is to be four I'd better lend a hand."

"Any contributions gratefully accepted," said Cole when he saw his friend enter the fray.

"Wait now, you fizzneless gomerils!" said the sandy-haired Scotsman. "'Tis not fair to sully a friendly boxing match with pistols and the like."

The closest hoodlums, a cream-colored man, was pulling a .38 revolver out of his checkered overcoat.

Mac's foot suddenly rose up.

The man with the gun cried out. The dour

MacMurdie had kicked the weapon from his hand.

Deftly sidestepping, Mac caught the gun as it came spinning down through the night darkness. "Now, me fine-feathered skurlies, we'll just—"

Someone gave him a ferocious shove from behind. Mac slammed into the side of a parked car, producing a great hollow thunk.

Before he got himself upright he heard the sedan doors slapping shut.

"Sorry, Mac," apologized Cole. "I forgot about the one I tossed into the wall." He was sitting on the sidewalk, rubbing his head.

The one-eyed man had come to, sapped Cole and pushed MacMurdie over. Then he and his sidekick had run for their car.

The sedan was roaring off down the street now. It went squealing around a corner and away.

Taking the proffered hand of the redhaired girl, Cole stood. "Look on the bright side, Mac. We saved this young lady from . . . it occurs to me, miss, that I'm not exactly sure who we saved you from. Who were those lads exactly?"

"I appreciate what you two have done," said the girl. "But I'm afraid I really can't tell you anything."

"Well, I like a woman of mystery," said Cole, grinning. "At least allow me to see you safely to your destination."

A truck came rumbling up the street, slowed

in front of MacMurdie's drugstore. A bundle of tied newspapers was tossed out.

The girl hesitated, then said, "I think I'm actually fairly close to the place I was looking for. Can you tell me how to find Fergus Mac-Murdie?"

MacMurdie laughed. "Lass, you've found him."

Cole gave the nozzle handle one more jerk. "MacMurdie keeps ignoring my suggestion that he serve champagne," he said as he handed the glass of sparkling water across the counter to the girl. "This will have to do."

The girl smiled at him. She was sitting on the stool Cole had vacated when he'd heard her scream. "I don't quite know," she said slowly, "how . . . how to begin. I don't even know if you'll be able to help me."

MacMurdie was absently slicing the cord that held the bundle of the first edition of tomorrow's newspaper. "You might commence, lass, by telling us who you are."

"My name is Lizbeth Kearny."

"I'm Cole Wilson," said the grinning Cole. "I didn't get a chance to thoroughly introduce myself during the recent brawl."

"Hush, mon, and let her tell her tale," admonished the Scot.

"Some friends of my father's once mentioned your name, Mr. MacMurdie," Lizbeth said. "They told me you helped people who were in trouble . . . or rather, that you were part of an organization that did."

MacMurdie set a copy of the newspaper up on the counter to read later. "Aye, we've had some luck in that direction."

"Judging from what just happened outside, I'd say you were the one in trouble," said Cole. "But when you mentioned your father you got a funny look in your eye."

The girl's attention had been attracted to something on the front page of the newspaper. She reached one slender hand out, turned it over to read another paragraph below the fold. "Excuse me. What were you asking me?"

"If your father's in trouble," repeated Cole.

The girl began to rummage in her black purse. "Darn," she said. "I must have dropped it in the street." She hopped from the stool. "Stay right here and I'll get it. That'll explain everything."

Before either of the two men could dissuade her, Lizbeth ran quickly out of the drugstore.

"She shouldn't go out there unprotected," Cole hurried from behind the counter.

"Oh, I doubt that crew of skurlies will make two tries this night."

Cole sprinted outside to the sidewalk. "Lizbeth," he called.

No one answered him.

For the very good reason that the street was empty.

CHAPTER II

The Man from Atlantis

The Avenger leaned forward and circled an item on the front page of the newspaper. "This must be it," he said in his level voice.

Cole Wilson was leaning with his hip against the edge of Dick Benson's desk. He narrowed his eyes, read the item's headline upside down. "'Man From Atlantis Collapses On Fifth Avenue.'" He shook his head, grinning a puzzled grin. "Looks like just one more silly season sort of story, Dick."

No expression touched the Avenger's face. He was a dark-haired young man of average height, his eyes almost colorless. And for one so young he seemed curiously somber. "Fill him in, Josh."

Joshua Elijah H. Newton, a lanky Negro, was

slouched in a soft chair across the room from the Avenger's desk. For the outside world Josh, an honor graduate from Tuskegee, played a part. But here, inside the top floor offices of Justice, Inc., he was himself. "About four months ago a crack research chemist named Dr. Norbert A. Kearny disappeared under mysterious circumstances," Josh said in the slow drawl he never quite abandoned.

"Woosh!" exclaimed MacMurdie. "He must be the lass's father."

"Dr. Kearny has two children," continued the black man. "A son, age twenty-six, named J. Randolph Kearny, now serving with the Air Corps, and a daughter, Lizbeth, age twenty-five."

"She looked hardly more than twenty-one," said Cole.

"They all do to you," said Nellie Gray. The pretty little blond girl had been sitting quietly, arms folded, while Mac and the grinning Cole had recounted their recent adventure with Lizbeth Kearny.

"Ah, there you are, pixie," said Cole. "I didn't notice you before. Must have been looking right over the top of your head."

Nellie wrinkled her nose by way of reply.

"I've heard of this herrre Kearny," said Mac, scratching at his sandy hair. "Rumored to be doing some very hush-hush government work, wasn't he?"

"Yes," said the Avenger. "I'm afraid we'll see

some pretty terrible weapons used before this war is over."

"Is that what Dr. Kearny was working on?" Cole asked.

"His main job," answered Josh, drawing on the encyclopedic amount of information he kept stored in his head, "was to work out defenses against the more sophisticated stuff the other side might come up with."

Mac asked, "How sophisticated now?"

"There are," said Dick Benson, his eyes flashing now with suppressed anger, "weapons much worse than guns or bombs, Mac. There are chemical weapons and even, though it may seem hard to believe any civilized country would resort to them, biological weapons—man-made plagues."

"I imagine then," said Cole as he moved across the room and dropped into a chair near Nellie, "our government must be pretty anxious to get Lizbeth's dear old dad back into the fold." He'd taken the newspaper and began to read the circled story.

"Not only our government," said the Avenger.

MacMurdie paced around the large office, bouncing, making small hemming sounds in his throat. He halted, saying, "This Kearny lass was obviously intending to come to us for help in finding her father."

"None of the government agencies or agents have been able to find a trace of him in over four months," said the black Josh.

"How did he disappear?" the dour Scot wanted to know.

"In the classic style," said Dick Benson. "He left his home one pleasant summer morning and went walking off down the street. No one has seen him since."

"And nobody, from the FBI on down," added Josh, "can trace him any farther than the corner of a half block from his home."

"Perhaps he found a way to turn himself invisible," said Mac.

Cole slapped the newspaper which rested across his knee. "Suppose Dr. Kearny came up with something that would knock a man down, like this man from Atlantis guy, and turn him green."

"That's a distinct possibility," said the Avenger in his unemotional voice.

"Maybe then," said Cole, "that's why you think this particular story is the one that caused Lizbeth to take off in such a hurry."

"I can think of other reasons," said Nellie out of the corner of her mouth.

Cole cupped his hand to his ear. "Hark, I think I heard an insult floating on the evening air."

Josh gave the two of them a mock scowl. "There's a more important reason for tying this newspaper story in with Kearny," he said. "He's one of the leading Atlantis scholars in the country."

"But this green guy isn't really from Atlantis," Cole said. "That's only a newspaper joke, be-

19

cause one of the witnesses thinks he heard him mutter something about Atlantis."

"The medallion," said Dick Benson.

Cole picked up the newspaper, scanned the account once more. " 'The green man, who carried no identification whatsoever, was holding a curious gold medallion. There is a representation of a three-pronged fork on one side and some cryptic writing on the other.' So?"

"That's the sign of Poseidon," explained Josh. "He's supposed to be the chief god worshiped in Atlantis. The Romans later took him over and called him Neptune."

"Hold on," said little Nellie. "You know darn well, Josh, that all this Atlantis stuff is nothing but a fairy tale. A myth made up thousands of years ago by . . . by Aristotle or somebody."

"Plato," said Josh.

"Well, I was close."

"Whether Atlantis once existed or not doesn't matter at the moment," said Dick Benson. "We have a missing scientist, a man who's very important to America's future, and we know for a fact he's a student of everything connected with the Atlantis legend. A man collapses on Fifth Avenue and no one has yet been able to determine the cause. This man is holding tight to a medallion which pertains to Atlantis. Lizbeth Kearny comes to Mac to ask us for help. When she sees this story in the paper about the so-called man from Atlantis she rushes away. That's too many coincidences."

"Says here this green lad was taken to the

Westlake Hospital in the West Fifties," said
Cole. "That's where Lizbeth must have headed."

"Look at his ears perk up," remarked Nellie.
"Reminds me of an old hunting dog my Uncle
Bud used to have."

"Well, now," said MacMurdie, rubbing his
hands together. "It seems like we've more or less
been invited into this little problem. Do we go
ahead and investigate?"

"We do," said the Avenger.

At that moment the door opened and a giant
came into the room carrying what appeared to
be, at first glance, a severed head.

"Happy Halloween," said the giant.

"A jack-o-lantern," exclaimed Nellie when
she realized what it actually was the huge man
was carrying so carefully in his big rough hands.

The name of the giant was Algernon Heathcote Smith, though very few people called him
that, more than once. To the circle of dedicated
crime fighters who worked with Dick Benson
the big man was simply Smitty. Smitty was a
specialist in the field of electrical engineering.
"Wouldn't be Halloween without a pumpkin I
figured," he said.

"That's an absolutely lovely piece of work,
Smitty," said the pretty blonde. Normally she
would have kidded the big man some, but tonight she was reserving her barbs for the grinning Cole Wilson.

While Smitty placed the carved pumpkin on
a coffee table near Nellie's chair and got the
candle inside it lit, Dick made a phone call.

His face showing nothing, the Avenger hung up after a few minutes of quiet conversation. He lifted the phone again to put through another call. It was also brief.

Though Benson's face did not indicate it, Mac sensed something was bothering him. "What is it?"

"I've just talked to the Westlake Hospital and the local FBI office," replied the Avenger.

"When can we see this green man?" asked Cole.

"According to both the hospital and the FBI," said Dick, "the newspaper story is a hoax. There is no such person as the man from Atlantis."

CHAPTER III

Neverwas

The crisp white-clad nurse seemed to be looking not at her but at a point about a foot and a half to her right. "I'm afraid I don't quite understand, miss," she said.

The redhaired Lizbeth Kearny stood with her hands pressing the edge of the hospital reception desk. "I don't know the man's name," she said, her voice showing she was struggling to keep her emotions under control. "I read the newspaper account in a hurry. I don't know if they even gave his name."

"Then the patient you wish to see is not a relative or close friend of yours?" The reception nurse had added to her eyebrows with an eyebrow pencil. The left one was a quarter inch wider than the right. "Is that it?"

"Yes, but he may know something about my father," said the anxious girl. "You must know the patient I mean. There can't have been many green men admitted here tonight."

The nurse's artificial eyebrows climbed up her face. "Beg pardon, miss?"

"The man, the patient I want to see, he was . . . didn't you see the story in the paper?"

"I'm afraid I don't quite understand, miss." The nurse turned so that she was facing away from the redheaded girl. "Maybe you ought to go home and sleep off your Halloween party."

Lizbeth looked anxiously around the pale green lobby of the Westlake Hospital. Near a bank of phone booths was a green metal newspaper rack. "I'll show you," she said, running to the rack.

A young doctor with rumpled blond hair stopped to watch Lizbeth searching her purse for a nickel. He joined her, said, "Allow me," and dropped a coin in the slot.

"Thanks." Lizbeth grabbed out a paper.

"You seem to be having trouble with our resident watchdog."

"Maybe you can help me," said the girl. "I have to see the man who was brought in here earlier tonight. The story is right here in the . . ." She didn't conclude her sentence. Reaching out, she ran her fingertips over the front page. "It . . . it's not here."

"Friend or relative in an accident?"

"No, it was the green man. I have to talk to him."

"Green man?"

Lizbeth's purse dropped to the floor as she unfurled the newspaper to search the inside pages. "They found him unconscious . . . on Fifth Avenue . . . brought him here. But I can't find the story in the paper anymore."

"Is this some kind of Halloween stunt? I mean, are you on a scavenger hunt or something like that?"

Lizbeth gave an exasperated sigh. "No, and I'm not drunk or crazy either. Can't you help me?"

"Be happy to." The young doctor bent and retrieved her purse for her. Then he guided her over to a leatherette sofa in the waiting room area. "Sit down and tell me all about it."

"Oh, get that patronizing tone out of your voice," said the girl angrily. "I don't want to be humored. I tell you there was a story in the paper about a man who collapsed on Fifth Avenue. He was holding onto a gold medallion that I know . . . well, never mind about that. I have to find out who the man is."

"And he was green you say? You mean he was madeup?"

"He was obviously a victim of . . . no, it wasn't makeup."

"A victim of what? I'm not familiar with any disease that will turn a man green. Yellow, yes, and sometimes pink but—"

"Can't you let me talk to whomever it was who admitted him?"

"I've been working in emergency admissions since six," the young doctor told her. "I can assure you we haven't had any green men come in. It's usually pretty dull down in emergency this early. Everybody would have noticed somebody like that. Only excitement was a kid who swallowed a half dozen of his mother's ration tokens. She was more interested in—"

"Who's in charge of the hospital?"

"You want to go over my head?" he asked with a laugh.

"This isn't, don't you understand, a joke," the girl insisted. "This man must know something about my father."

"You could talk to Dr. Pronzini," said the young man. "He's in charge of things this time of night." He stood up. "Got his office right down the hall here. I'll show you."

"Thanks."

After the young doctor escorted Lizbeth to the office in question he came back to the lobby. Stepping into a phone booth, he dropped a nickel in the slot and gave the operator a local number.

When the phone was answered on the other end he said, "Extension 1000 please."

After several seconds a voice said, "Go ahead."

"M270."

"Proceed."

"She's here now. They're giving her the runaround, as anticipated. She's in talking with one of the doctors."

"For how long?"

"No way of telling, but I wouldn't guess very long."

"We'll take action."

The blond young man hung up and left the booth. He crossed the lobby and walked out into the night.

Dr. Pronzini was a chain smoker, a fat mottled man in his early sixties. He jiggled in his swivel chair. "I'm afraid, Miss Kearny, you've been the victim of a joke," he said, exhaling swirls of smoke with his words.

"But the newspaper story—"

"Somebody's idea of a joke, prompted by the fact this is Halloween no doubt. As you've noticed the later editions have dropped it."

Lizbeth clasped her hands together until the tips of her fingers grew white. "It's been so long . . . I thought finally there might be some lead to my father."

The fat doctor jiggled a few more times. "I don't see exactly how this particular hoax story connects with your missing father."

"I can't tell you all the . . . the medallion mentioned. It sounded very much like one my father acquired shortly before his disappearance."

"I see." Dr. Pronzini lit a new Lucky Strike from the butt of the old one. "It is an odd coincidence, isn't it? But perhaps, in your anxiety to find your father, you clutched at a straw."

"The medallion described in the story has to be the same one." She pushed back her chair, got up. "I simply don't believe, if the story is a joke, that the details are simply due to a coincidence. I'm going to talk to someone at the newspaper office."

"Let me give you some free advice, which I don't often do." Pronzini, with considerable wheezing, rose up to see her out. "Forget about this green man. There never was such a person. That's all you'll learn from the paper."

"Thank you, doctor."

"I've read several of your father's books, Miss Kearny." He opened the door. "I admire him very much."

"So do I." Lizbeth walked rapidly down the corridor and out of the hospital. Since the newspaper offices were only blocks away, she decided to walk rather than wait for a hard-to-get taxi.

As she came down the hospital steps the headlights of a car parked down the block flashed on and then off.

Lizbeth didn't notice.

CHAPTER IV

Death in White

Richard Henry Benson still sat behind his big desk. He was, except for the slowly drumming fingers of his left hand, completely immobile. "Our green man is apparently important to others beside Miss Kearny," he said.

"Maybe it is only a joke," suggested the huge Smitty. "Lot of goofy stuff turns up in the papers, what with propaganda and rumors and all."

"Details," said the Avenger.

"There were enough specifics in that account," elaborated Josh, "to convince the Kearny girl"

"Unless," said Nellie, "she's a hoax, too."

"She was real enough," said Cole, "and in real trouble."

MacMurdie was sitting on the edge of a chair,

knees going rapidly up and down. "I say we ought to do something," he put in. "This lass, poor fatherless bairn, was coming to Justice, Inc. for help. So let's be up and helping her."

"You're as smitten as Cole," observed Nellie. "You're not your usual dour self, Fergus."

MacMurdie rubbed a rough finger along the side of his nose. "By the sacred bones of the Black Douglas, lass, I know real danger when I smell it."

The Avenger's fingers ceased drumming. "Here's what we'll do," he said in his level voice.

Benson had founded the efficient crime-fighting squad known as Justice, Inc. to destroy crime and to aid those in need of help, especially those the normal arms of the law could or would not help. He was particularly attracted to seemingly puzzling events. And nothing could have made him more interested in the problem of Lizbeth Kearny than the fact someone was trying to cover up things. This was a challenge to the Avenger.

"The green man had to come from someplace," he said now to Josh. "He was first noticed in Grand Central station. Find out where he was before that."

"Yep." The lanky black man stretched to his feet and eased out of the big office.

"You have friends in the newspaper game, Cole," continued Benson. "Get over to Times Square and see what you can learn."

"I'd learn more if I tried to pick up the girl, or her trail, at the Westlake Hospital," said Cole.

Benson said, "I'll be checking out the setup there."

Nellie stuck her tongue into her cheek, gave the departing Cole a small farewell wave.

The Avenger stood up. "The rest of you stand by," he told his remaining associates. With that he strode from the room.

The crisp reception nurse looked up as a medium-sized dark-haired young doctor came walking across the lobby of the Westlake Hospital. He carried a black medical bag in his left hand.

"I'm Dr. Benson," said the Avenger. "I have to see Dr. Pronzini at once."

"Oh, yes, doctor." She left her chair, leaned over the counter and pointed. "You'll find his office right down there. Shall I alert anyone for you?"

"That won't be necessary."

The heavyset doctor was shaking out a match when Benson pushed open the door of his office. "Yes, what is it?" he asked after a quick puff on his Lucky.

"I'm Dr. Benson." The Avenger set his black bag on the edge of Dr. Pronzini's desk.

The older man exhaled tatters of smoke. "Should I have heard of you, doctor?"

The Avenger, his almost colorless eyes on the seated man, opened the black bag and thrust in his hand. "Mine is a very specialized practice."

"Then perhaps you'll—"

Benson was pointing a strange weapon at him.

It was something like a piece of blued steel tubing, bent slightly at one end to form a handle. This was the special silenced gun Benson called Mike. Despite its unconventional design the doctor recognized it at once as a gun, a gun pointed directly at his head. "I'd like some information," said the Avenger.

Dr. Pronzini coughed out smoke. "The drugs are all locked up. As for money—"

"I want to see the green man."

"Uh . . . green man, did you say?"

"Where have you got him?"

"We don't have—"

The Avenger's eyes flashed as he leaned closer to the doctor. "Where?"

"He's on three," answered Dr. Pronzini. He's in 301. But there's a guard at the door. You'll—"

"Who's inside the room with him?"

"No one at the moment I believe. We're waiting for Dr. Reisberson to arrive from Stamford General. He's an expert in . . . uh . . . in this sort of case."

Benson didn't follow that up. He had a fairly good idea of what the man from Atlantis was suffering from. "What about the medallion?"

"It's . . . it's still in his hand. He wouldn't let go of it."

"Who ordered you to deny the man was here?"

"Everyone," replied the heavyset doctor. "FBI . . . New York police . . . some man from Washington."

Benson reached out and touched a certain spot on the doctor's neck. "Thank you for your help."

Dr. Pronzini slumped forward, his head landing in his overflowing ashtray.

The Avenger left the office.

The husky cop moved his right hand toward his holster as Benson approached the door of 301. "No admittance," he announced.

"Nonsense, nonsense," said Benson in an impatient nasal voice. "I'm Dr. Reisberson and I certainly didn't rush here all the way from Stamford, Connecticut, to be turned away by some hulking minion of the law."

"Sorry, doctor." The policeman moved his gun hand up to touch the visor of his cap.

"Yes, yes. Now get out of the way." The Avenger grabbed the doorknob, turned it and went into the green man's room.

There was a strong smell of drugs and disinfectants in the white room. A series of white screens hid the patient's bed.

Benson was ten feet from the bed when one of the screens began to sway. It toppled over.

A man in a black overcoat was bent over the man in the white bed.

"No you don't!" Benson sprinted forward.

The man turned, threw a bloody silver knife at the charging Avenger.

Benson dodged. The knife whizzed by his head.

The man in the black overcoat shoved the bed at him now. Then he dived for the open window.

Unable to get out of the way quite fast enough, the Avenger was bowled off his feet. As he hit the floor he heard footsteps clattering away down the fire escape.

The green man began to fall out of the bed. There was an awful grin frozen on his face. His throat had been cut, the bright red blood contrasting horribly with the green of his skin.

The man from Atlantis fell atop the Avenger, splashing him with blood.

"What's going on in . . . ?" A nurse had stepped into the room. She commenced screaming. "My lord, he's killed him! Help, he's killed him!"

CHAPTER V

Scarecrow

A cluster of sailors whistled at her. Lizbeth Kearny continued walking briskly along war-dimmed Broadway. She was only two blocks from the offices of the newspaper.

Three young men, all a few months short of draft age, were approaching her from the opposite direction. They walked side by side, arms locked, weaving slightly. Each wore a domino mask and a paper hat.

Lizbeth did not slow.

A second before they would have collided with her the boys broke rank, allowing her to pass.

"Oh, Red!" called one of them at her trim retreating back.

While the girl waited at the next corner for

the light to change, a tattered figure lurched out of a darkened doorway.

The man had a cloth head, a fuzzy grin painted on it. Straw flickered out of rents in his sleeves. Catching hold of the brim of his floppy black hat with both gloved hands the scarecrow tottered toward the curb.

The light went green, Lizbeth hurried across.

"Where'd that damn yellow brick road go?" mumbled the scarecrow.

Getting a tighter grip on her purse, Lizbeth increased her pace. She could see the lights of the newspaper offices half a block ahead of her.

A strange sound began behind her. A shuffling, crackling sound.

"Miss Kearny, isn't it?"

She spun, saw the scarecrow was only a few inches behind her. "What do you want?"

"Merely a few words with you, Miss Kearny." His voice had a droning, murmuring quality behind the rough painted cloth which masked his face.

"Some other time. I—"

"Now's as good a time as any, Miss Kearny." He grabbed hold of her arm with a gloved hand. Straw sprinkled out of his cuff.

"Let go."

The other hand touched her arm. Something jabbed through the cloth of her coat, bit hard into the flesh of her upper arm. "I'd like you to come along with me, Miss Kearny."

"No, I—" Lizbeth found she could no longer speak. She wanted to struggle, desired desperately to cry out for help. But she could do nothing.

"We'll just walk around the corner to our car, Miss Kearny."

The girl obeyed.

Cole Wilson was whistling. Whistling didn't cost anything, it didn't use any materials that were essential to the war effort. All in all, an admirable pastime. Although, as a matter of fact, he'd rather be spending his time with that pretty redheaded Lizbeth Kearny. "Relax, old chum," he told himself as he walked up Broadway toward the newspaper offices. "It's all in the lap of the gods. Fate brought us together once, it'll do it again. Be optimistic, which is the code of the Wilsons."

A pair of adolescent girls, one dressed in the costume of a princess and the other shivering in a gaudy sarong, giggled in his direction as they emerged from a coffee shop.

"I'm already spoken for," grinned Cole. Then his attention was attracted by something a block away. He spotted a man in a scarecrow costume leading a girl by the arm. They turned off Broadway.

"Whoosh, to paraphrase Mac, if that doesn't look like the missing Lizbeth." He broke into a swift run.

A green coupe, motor idling, was the scarecrow's destination. The door on the passenger side swung open to receive the redhaired girl and the straw-stuffed man.

"Hold it, folks," called Cole. He was only yards from the auto.

"It's the guy from the drugstore," said the scarecrow, pausing in the act of shoving Lizbeth into the machine.

Suddenly the rumble seat popped open. A man in a gorilla suit rose up. He clutched a .45 automatic.

"Wait'll Darwin hears about this." Cole dived for the gutter as the gun fired.

The slug missed him. He rolled.

"Inside, Miss Kearny." The scarecrow gave her a push.

The redhaired girl tumbled into the car.

The gorilla man tried another shot.

Cole was rolling and tumbling too rapidly to make a good target.

Around on Broadway a woman screamed, a man shouted.

"What the hell?"

"Guns. It's guns!"

"It's the Germans!"

"It's the Japs!"

"An invasion. It's an invasion!"

Cole sprang to his feet. He threw himself at the scarecrow. He got a firm grip on the man's arm, twisted him around and put him between himself and the gorilla with a gun. "Come on out, Lizbeth," invited Cole.

The girl did not move, did not even look in his direction.

Cole sensed someone behind him. He jerked his head around.

It was the one-eyed man he'd tangled with earlier in front of MacMurdie's. Snarling, the man jabbed something into Cole's arm.

Cole was going to make one of his grinning responses. He couldn't seem to say anything. The world went blurry. The one-eyed man, the scarecrow, the gorilla all faded away.

Everything was gone and there was only darkness.

There was blue on every side of the Avenger. Four uniformed policemen, three with service revolvers drawn, circled him near the doorway of the green man's room.

A fifth cop was bent over the dead man. "Too late," he announced. "This guy's dead and done for."

"Why'd you knock him off?" asked one of the policemen with a gun.

The Avenger was an impossible man to intimidate. He did not cringe, give ground, or attempt to explain anything. "Who's in charge of this case?" he asked in his level voice.

"We'll ask the questions, buddy."

Bluster didn't seem to work on this average-sized man with the colorless eyes. Slowly, the cops backed away a little from him. The man without the gun rubbed the sole of one black shoe over the floor of the hospital room.

"Lt. Coe's the one who's in charge of watching this guy," he told Benson now.

"Get him," suggested the Avenger.

"Who do you . . . ?" began one of the other policemen. He decided, for some reason, not to finish the sentence. He cleared his throat, dropped his gun back in its black leather holster. "He's on his way up anyhow. He was having a cup of coffee down with some of the docs."

Benson nodded his head once. He took a step back from the uniformed men, folded his arms.

The fifth cop, stepping gingerly to avoid any of the splashed blood, examined the window. "Appears like he had help," he said to his companions. "Somebody climbed out this window."

One of the others shook his head. "We should of had somebody out there."

"We should have done a lot of things better," said the stocky man who pushed his way into the room. "Okay, I don't need all you bums in here. Olsen, stick around. Tully, see if anybody saw a guy come down the fire escape into that alley down there. The rest of you, make yourselves useful elsewhere."

"Good evening, Lieutenant," said the Avenger.

Coe jabbed a hand into a wrinkled pocket of the gray overcoat he was wearing. He took out a pack of cigarettes that had been torn down the middle, plucked out one and thrust it between his lips. "According to what I heard, Benson," he said, "you were supposed to be anyplace but here."

"How much do you know about this man?"

Coe found a book of paper matches in the same wrinkled coat pocket and lit his cigarette. "Nothing I can tell you," he said. "You told my man you were a doctor, huh?"

"It's a good serviceable guise to assume when in a hospital," said Benson.

The police lieutenant walked away from the Avenger, went and looked at the dead man. "Nasty," he said. He noticed the severed fingers. "Why'd they mutilate him?"

"To get the medallion," said Benson.

Coe spit out a cloud of smoke. "I don't like these screwy ones," he said. "It was bad enough he was green . . . now somebody climbs in a window and cuts his throat to steal some old gold coin."

"It's more important than that."

Coe turned away from the corpse. "You seem to know a hell of a lot about this, Benson." He lifted his left foot, flicked ashes into the cuff of his trousers. "I know a lot of guys around Centre Street think you're terrific. Me . . ." He shrugged.

"Would you like a description of the man who did the killing?"

"You saw him, huh?"

"He was finishing up when I walked in," said Benson. "As you've probably noticed there was a struggle. Unfortunately the man got away."

"Olsen," said the lieutenant, "get your book and take down what Mr. Richard Henry Benson has to tell us."

The cop's face brightened. "Oh, you're *that* Benson," he said.

While Benson was telling the cop what he'd seen the door opened. Another plainclothesman came in. He gave the Avenger a quick nod, took Lt. Coe off into the corner of the room with him. The two policemen talked for three minutes. The plainclothesman gave Benson another brief nod and left.

Lt. Coe flicked more ashes into his cuff. "Somebody else wants to see you, Benson," he said. "My detective is waiting out in the hall to take you there."

"Who wants to see me?"

"I'm not even sure," answered Coe. "Some kind of big muckymuck government guy. He's using a room on one of the other floors as a temporary office." More smoke came swirling out of his mouth and nose. "I hate these screwy ones."

CHAPTER VI

Keep Out—This Means You!

The clean cut young man handed Benson another fresh white towel. "Little splash of blood just under your ear," he said amiably. "There, you've got it."

The two of them were in a bare white room somewhere in the Westlake Hospital. There was a white porcelain sink, a hanging overhead lamp. The Avenger studied the young man, his eyes seeming to burn into the close-cropped blond head. "Who are you?" he asked.

"Name's Don Early." He was tall, lean, wearing a wrinkled tweed suit and carrying a tan raincoat over his arm.

"You're not with the New York police," said Benson, "nor the FBI."

"That's right," admitted Early. "Know all

about you, though. You've had a very impressive career to date, Mr. Benson."

"A stone wall," said the Avenger. "Somebody's trying to build one between me and this case."

"There is no case," said Early.

"And no dead man up there in 301?"

"Matter of fact, no. Body's been removed by now."

Benson began to pace the white room. He appeared calm outwardly, yet there was something suggestive of a caged tiger about him. "Who exactly are you working for, Early?"

"We're on the same side," Early assured him. "I work for a federal agency which looks into odd and unusual problems."

"So you know what the man in 301 was suffering from."

"Prior to his slit throat? Yeah, I do."

"Then it should be evident to you he had some contact with Kearny or those who hold him."

"Possibility," admitted the government man in his amiable way. "Thing is, Mr. Benson, we don't want you to worry about any of this anymore."

"You expect me to walk in on a murder," demanded the Avenger, "and then forget all about it?"

"Be nice if you would, yes." Early pointed. "Little speck of blood on your wrist there."

"You've been instructed to tell me to forget all about the man from Atlantis. Is that it?"

"About the size of it."

"How high up?" Benson again turned his glowing eyes on him. "Did the President himself request it?"

"Not quite that high up, but high enough."

"I see," said Benson. "I hope you realize what you're fooling with here, Early."

"Think I got a pretty good idea."

"The man in the black overcoat," said the Avenger, "got the gold medallion."

"Figured that's why he cut off a few of that fellow's fingers." It was an hour now since the Avenger had seen the green man killed. The plainclothes cops who'd come to investigate the murder knew who he was. But they'd been reluctant to talk to him. Early had appeared a few minutes after the police and requested a private interview with Benson. "Let us worry about that."

"The medallion belonged to Kearny."

"Could be." Early walked to the door. "Hope you'll give me your promise to forget all about what happened here, Mr. Benson. Your statement will be a lot of help, I'm sure." He turned the knob.

"I don't forget murder." Benson crossed the room.

"The stone walls can get higher and thicker."

The Avenger said nothing more. He left the white room.

Gray dawn showed at the office windows. Dick Benson rose from behind his desk and walked to a window to gaze reflectively down on Bleek Street. The windows appeared to be shielded by Venetian blinds, but actually these were disguised slats of bulletproof steel through which the Avenger stared.

The Avenger owned the entire block. One side was taken up with the windowless backside of a concrete warehouse. On this side were several stores and small storage buildings in the center of which stood three narrow dingy brick buildings which had once been rooming houses. These formed a façade which hid the modern expansive headquarters of Justice, Inc.

Benson's eyes narrowed as he observed the giant Smitty come tromping along the early morning sidewalk. The huge man was alone, a dejected look on his face and a forlorn droop to his massive shoulders.

When Smitty came into the office the Avenger was again seated behind his desk. He had been there most of the night.

"Still no word, huh?" asked the giant as he slumped dejectedly into a chair.

"Nothing."

They had heard no word from Cole Wilson since the night before. The Avenger had dispatched various of his aides to find some clue.

Smitty rested his big knobby hands on his knees. "Well, I think I found out what happened to Cole," he said, "but I don't know where he is."

"What have you learned?"

The big man shifted his position, scratching

at his ribs. "First off, he never got as far as the newspaper office," began Smitty. "From what I've been able to piece together, Cole was snatched just off Broadway at around twelve last night. Several guys were involved, and a green coupe. We're not likely to find out much about what the guys looked like, since they were wearing trick suits."

"Halloween costumes?"

"Yeah, one was got up like a scarecrow, another was decked out in a gorilla suit."

"We should be able to trace the costumes, if we have to."

Nodding, Smitty continued. "Then there was some shooting," he told Benson, "but it doesn't look like anybody got hurt."

"They were firing at Cole?"

"Yeah, and maybe at the Kearny girl," answered Smitty. "A redhaired dame was there at the scene, according to the witnesses."

"What became of Cole and the girl?"

"There are at least two theories about that. A couple of the witnesses told the police the scarecrow and the gorilla heaved the redhead and Cole into the coupe. Drove away with them," explained the big man. "One old gal insists she saw several Japanese soldiers carry them off. That sounds like war jitters."

"You went over the site?"

"Sure, and Cole didn't leave anything behind for us."

"What about the car?"

"No license plates," said Smitty. "Some guy

says he saw a B gas rationing sticker in the window, for what that's worth."

The Avenger said, "Cole may be able to get word to us. Meantime we'll—"

A tiny bubble of red light glowed from the wall beside the doorway. This meant someone had rung the bell on the street door downstairs.

Dick Benson pushed a button which allowed the lower door to open. He then flicked a switch and a television screen near his large desk bloomed to light. On the screen showed a grim-faced white haired man in a chrome wheelchair. This television screen, an invention of Smitty's, gave the Avenger a sharp, clear view of anyone who appeared in the foyer below.

"Hey, isn't that—?" asked the big Smitty.

"Yes, it's Asa Grimshaw," said Dick, "the Secretary of the Navy."

As they watched, MacMurdie also came into the lobby.

Moments later the door of the Avenger's top-floor office was opened.

"Allow me to push you to an advantageous position, sir," offered the sandy-haired Scot, who was immediately behind the crippled cabinet member.

"That won't be necessary, young man." Grimshaw was a leathery old man; from the waist up he looked like a tough outdoor type. His legs, however, were frail and twisted. He rolled himself close to Benson's desk. "You're looking well, Richard."

"I didn't know you were in New York, Asa."

"You weren't supposed to," said the Secretary. "I don't give out my itinerary these days." He rested his sinewy hands on the silver arms of his wheelchair, glancing around the large room. "You're Fergus MacMurdie. I've heard a great deal about some of the things you've come up with."

" 'Tis nothing much really."

"And you're Algernon Heathcote Smith."

Smitty's respect for the reputation of the Navy Secretary kept him from resenting the use of his disliked full name. "Yes, sir."

"I don't suppose they usually call you that, though."

"Smitty," said Smitty, "is what they usually call me."

"Smitty it shall be then," said Grimshaw. "I've heard a good many favorable things about your work as well."

The Avenger's calm, even voice said, "You didn't come here this early in the morning simply to pass out compliments, Asa."

"This isn't early for me, Richard. Since . . . since I took to riding in this gadget I seldom sleep beyond 5:00 A.M." He caught hold of the chair wheels, backed off a few feet from Benson. "But you're right, I have another reason for my visit. I came to ask you a favor, you and Justice, Inc. You've done many admirable things, Richard, helped your country, and you've had the nerve to go into places where others fear to tread. But now—"

49

"Does this have to do with the man from Atlantis?" asked the Avenger.

For a few seconds new wrinkles, lines of surprise, appeared on the Secretary's weatherworn face. They faded, replaced by a faint smile. "Yes, Richard," he answered. "It's come to my attention that you've taken an interest in this matter. Now let me reiterate the fact that the work done by you and your staff is most highly regarded. Highly regarded in a great many places in Washington, including the White House."

"Are you going to ask me to drop the matter, Asa?"

"That's exactly what I am going to do." The Secretary of the Navy hunched his shoulders slightly, causing the metal wheelchair to rattle. "I'm requesting, mind you, not ordering."

Very slowly the Avenger stood up. "Last night I said I wouldn't quit," he said. "This morning it looks as though one of my own people is in danger. I'm going to stick."

CHAPTER VII

Near Miss

Cole Wilson sniffed the air. "We're close to the Hudson River," he decided.

"How long," asked the redhaired girl, "do you think we were unconscious?"

Glancing toward the single boarded window far across the room, Cole said, "That looks like rosy fingered dawn trying to poke its way through the cracks. So I'd guess we were out all night."

Lizbeth Kearny asked, "How did they get hold of you?"

"It wasn't difficult for them, I more or less volunteered for the job."

They had both awakened moments earlier to find themselves alone in an unfurnished room. The faded hardwood floor was thick with dust in the untrod places, cigarette butts abounded along with chewing gum wrappers from the prewar years. Both Cole and the girl were tied hand and foot with fresh yellow rope.

"Where were you when they got you?" Lizbeth asked. She was sitting with her slim back against a smudgy plaster wall.

"Then you don't remember anything about my gallant rescue attempt?"

The pretty redhead frowned. "I have . . . a very faint recollection of your running . . . of someone shooting." She shook her head. "Everything is pretty hazy."

"The drug was already taking effect when I barged onto the scene."

"Had you been following me?"

Cole said, "No, Lizbeth. My heart was heavy, as a matter of fact, because I thought I'd never see you again. My native optimism, on the other hand, told me to let fate work her usual tricks. And, lo, there you were all at once being dragged along Broadway."

"What were you doing there?"

"On my way to query some of my journalistic cronies," he answered. "Were you aiming for the newspaper, too?"

Lizbeth hesitated, then said, "Yes."

"What about the hospital?"

"Hospital?"

"The Westlake Hospital," he said, "where they allegedly had the man from Atlantis."

The girl's eyes widened. "How did . . . how did you know I went there?"

"A bit of elementary detective work," said the grinning Cole. "I take it you didn't find out anything about your father at the hospital?"

"You Justice, Inc. people are as clever as I heard you were."

"Some of us." He shifted position, began trying to move his hands.

"Well, the people at the hospital treated me as though I were . . . well, either drunk or crazy or maybe a mixture of both. They claimed they'd had no patient such as the one the paper described, that the story was only some kind of Halloween hoax."

"We experienced similar denials."

"But why?"

"You should know that better than I," said Cole. "Your father was engaged in some kind of hush-hush government work. His bosses, whomever they are, obviously picked up the same clues from that newspaper yarn as you did. They moved faster." He found that he could get his left hand to move from his side a little. "And they want to keep this thing quiet."

"I really thought I had a lead finally," she said. "It's been so long . . . four months may not seem a long time, but when you're waiting for someone, just waiting."

"You've talked to the government haven't you?"

"Oh, yes. To the FBI and several other of the initial outfits," she said. "I've even been to Washington twice."

"I hear it's hard to find a hotel room there."

"It was, both times. Lot of good it did . . . all I got were polite assurances. Everything was being done that could be done, my father was bound to turn up soon." She gave an exasperated sigh. "Honestly, I don't know if they know any more than I do or not."

"That's the advantage of a polite government poker face." Cole'd been able to move his hand several inches, though it meant rubbing his wrist raw on the harsh rope. "They never give anything away."

She became, finally, aware of what he was doing. "Do you think you can—?"

"Keep making conversation," he told her in a low voice. Louder he said, "What about the medallion?"

"I'm certain it was father's. At least it sounded very much like the one he'd acquired shortly before he disappeared."

"Know how and where he acquired it?"

"No, from some curio dealer I imagine," she replied. "I feel badly about it now, but I sometimes didn't pay that close attention to my father when he talked about his Atlantis hobby. I do know about the medallion, though, because he was quite excited about it. In fact, he had it with him when he left the house . . . on that day when he never came back."

Each of the Avenger's crew carried a compact two-way radio built into their belt buckle. Cole, slowly and painfully, was working his left hand toward the device so that he could activate it. "You're sure about that?"

"Yes, because he was planning on lunching with one of his fellow lost continent enthusiasts." In a soft quiet voice she asked, "What are you trying to do?"

"Got a miniature radio set in my belt," he explained in a whisper. "If I can flick it on we'll be able to call for help."

"I see." Lizbeth looked away from Cole, toward the unpainted wooden door of the room. Turning her head toward the door, she shouted out, "Come in here quick! He's trying to call the police! Hurry!"

CHAPTER VIII

Trails

"It's going to be tough," observed Smitty.

"Mon, don't be such a gloomy sairpuss," advised MacMurdie.

The Secretary of the Navy had taken his leave several minutes ago. They had been discussing his visit since.

"We've always cooperated with the government," said the giant man, "they've always cooperated with us. Now we got the Navy and some cloak and dagger guy telling us to lay off."

Benson had told them of his encounter with Don Early at the Westlake Hospital.

"We aren't for sure going to abandon Cole," said Mac. "If helping him means offending a few of the brasshats, so be it."

"The sooner," said the Avenger, "we get to the

men behind this whole thing, the sooner we find Cole and the Kearny girl."

The door to the large office opened. "I think I got us a lead on . . ." Josh stopped, noticing the faces of Smitty and the Scot. "What's wrong?"

"Cole's been snatched by a band of skurlies," said Mac.

"And the Secretary of the Navy doesn't want us to do anything about it," added Smitty.

"Secretary of the Navy?" said the black man as he crossed the room.

They told him what had been happening.

Then Benson said, "What did you find out about our green man?"

"Quite a lot." Josh sat down. "As you probably guessed, he wasn't always green. When he boarded his train he was a normal pink color."

"You know where he got on the train?"

"Yep, he came from a little town in Westchester County. Town name of Wollterville."

"Good work," said Smitty.

Josh shrugged. "All I did was talk to a few porters and a couple redcaps I know. The porter on the Atlantis guy's train noticed him when he got out, because he was staggering some and he figured him for a drunk."

"Had he seen the man before?" asked Benson.

"Nope, and he's a regular on that line," replied the Negro. "So this green man is maybe not a resident of Wollterville."

"You say, mon, he nae was green when he came aboard," put in Mac, "but he got off green.

Didn't it cause a commotion when he turned green?"

"He spent a lot of time in the washroom," said Josh. "When he came out that bright green shade everybody must have figured he put on makeup. There were a few kids on the train with funny hats and masks."

"Did the man say anything, do anything that would give some clue to his identity?" asked Benson.

"Toward the end of the trip he was mumbling to himself. My contact heard him say the word Atlantis several times. Actually he thought the guy was saying Atlantic." Josh leaned forward. "The porter saw the man arrive at the Wollterville station in a cab. So we might be able to pick up his trail that way. It's a small town."

"Who else has questioned this porter?" Benson asked.

"Nobody yet, but there were two plainclothes cops and a couple FBI boys descending on Grand Central when I was leaving," said Josh. "I carried some old woman's suitcase outside for her and got away without anybody spotting me. Protective coloration."

"Let's be off to Wollterville then," suggested Mac.

"Josh and I will handle that end of things," the Avenger told him.

"I'll call Rosabel and tell her I'm going out of town," said Josh.

"How's the lass feeling?" asked Mac.

"Pretty good, except for a little upset stomach mornings," answered Josh.

"That's to be expected."

Rosabel was Josh Newton's pretty wife. Until a few weeks ago she had worked actively with Justice, Inc.

"Don't be too specific with Rosabel about where we're going," cautioned Benson. "It's possible someone may be listening in."

"You think so?"

"We don't have time to check out all the phones now," said the Avenger. "But it's best to operate under the assumption we're under surveillance."

Josh laughed. "By the FBI? Boy, it's usually the guys on the other side who're trying to keep tabs on us."

Smitty cracked his big knuckles with a resounding crack. "You got something else in mind for us?" he asked the Avenger.

"The green man was carrying a gold medallion, muttering about Atlantis," said Benson. "He came to New York for some purpose. Perhaps that purpose was to find out more about that medallion. You and Mac talk to the people he might have been planning to see. Find out if any of them had an appointment with him."

"Which people might that be?" asked Mac-Murdie.

"Only a couple for you to check out," said Josh. "The most prominent Atlantis scholars in Manhattan, besides the missing Dr. Kearny himself, are Dr. Oscar Taverner and Professor Barry

Newgrass. Newgrass teaches at New York Experimental College, so he's likely to be in town. Taverner lectures now and then at a college in Westchester, meaning you may not catch him in."

Mac stood up. "I'm in the mood for action and the punching of a few skurlies and instead I'm to be doing academic work."

"You never know what your researches may turn up, Mac," said Dick Benson.

The truck bounced, milk cans rattled.

Cole Wilson studied the gunman who was sitting in a folding chair a few feet from him. "Yes, I've decided you looked better when you were wearing your gorilla suit."

The thickset man moved his .45 automatic an inch farther along his knee.

The redhaired Lizbeth, still securely bound, was seated on the closed truck's metal floor, wedged between two tarnished twenty-gallon milk cans. "I don't think you understand why I did what I did," she said across at Cole.

Cole, who was now minus his belt and buckle radio, said, "It's perfectly clear, make that *painfully* clear. You decided to be a Mata Hari. What I don't get is why they've still got you trussed up. Doesn't seem like a fitting reward for betraying me."

"What you don't comprehend at all," she said, contrition and vexation mixing in her voice, "is my reason for acting the way I did."

"Agreed," said Cole. "If I had my hands free at the moment I'd rub the new welts I have on my head right now."

"I didn't know they'd hit you like that."

The man with the automatic on his knee laughed without opening his mouth.

"How did you think they'd hit me?" asked Cole.

"What I mean is, I didn't expect them to hurt you at all," explained Lizbeth. "But I didn't want you getting us rescued just yet."

"Just yet?" echoed Cole. "Getting one's fat pulled out of the fire isn't something you can schedule like a lunch date or a visit to the Stork Club. You may have thrown away our only chance, woman."

"But don't you see that these people are probable the ones who took my father. That means," said Lizbeth, "we're more than likely being taken to where he is. I'll be able to see him again."

Cole chewed at the inside of his cheek. "Well, Lizbeth, I have to admit that walking into the lion's den has proved to be a successful technique for Richard Henry Benson. It remains to be seen whether it will work for us."

"Don't bet on it," said the man with the gun.

There was a piano playing down the hall, lights showing behind some of the pebbled glass doors. The brown linoleum of the hallway was worn, strewn with cigarette butts, gum wrappers. The lettering on the door said W&W Music Publishing, but that didn't mean anything.

The clean cut young man in the rumpled tweed suit opened the door. He crossed the darkened reception room, which smelled of old cigarettes and some kind of fly spray they'd used back in the Thirties.

Don Early flung his tan overcoat down on the bedraggled reception room sofa as he went by. He opened another door, crossed into a larger office. This one smelled a little better, but not much. "I wish we'd meet someplace that wasn't sleazy once in awhile," he said.

There was a thin man with short cut gray hair sitting in the straightback chair next to the battered desk. He held an unlit pipe in his right hand, his elbow rested on the edge of the desk. "We're not handling this one too well," he said. His voice had a raw worn out sound, as though he'd been yelling a lot.

Early went over and sat on the stool in front of the upright piano. "No," he agreed.

"How much does Benson know?"

"A lot more than he's willing to confide in me."

The other man tapped the stem of the pipe against his teeth. "I was hoping the polite warnings would keep him off this."

Early stuck his hands down into the pockets of his tweed slacks. "Don't think I'm being insubordinate, sir, but—"

"Don't go calling me sir."

"Excuse me." Early smiled very briefly. "What

I was going to say is . . . I don't see why we don't let the Avenger do what he wants. He's sure got a good track record."

The gray-haired man said, "I only work here, Don. Orders are he's not to get involved in this one. I'm not actually sure where the orders originated, but from pretty high up. As I've already told you."

"I know," said Early, turning around to frown at the keyboard. "The last few hours I've been getting the feeling I don't even know what's really going on."

"A war's going on."

"So I've heard. That's what my butcher tells me when I ask for steak." Early pressed down a few piano keys, but so gently they made no sound.

"You ought to know, Don, that the part of the war that goes on out in the open is only a small part of the whole picture."

"Yeah, I know, the tip of the iceberg."

"Maybe I have given you this lecture before. It's worth repeating." The gray-haired man bit down on the pipe stem. "Don't worry . . . I'm not going to give you a lot of cloak and dagger malarkey. But just remember, Don, that there are some pretty important things involved in this particular case. Professor Kearny was working on something pretty special, as you know. We have to get him back."

Early played another silent chord. "Seems to me Richard Benson would be able to help."

"Perhaps, but the word is to keep him out,"

said the gray-haired government agent. "Now, the question is . . . do you think he will?"

"I doubt it," replied Early.

The other man set the pipe down on the desk top with a click. "I'm not authorized to do anything further at the moment," he said. "But if the Avenger doesn't stop interfering, we may have to take steps to stop him."

"That's not going to be easy," said the clean cut young man.

CHAPTER IX

Boom!

The tortoise-shell cat eyed MacMurdie. It was perched on a nearly man-high pile of carbon copies and manuscript pages. When the brown and gold cat swished its tail the stack of last century books beside it swayed.

"I couldna work in such a clutter," Mac said in a low voice to Smitty.

The big man was about to reply when a door across the cluttered study opened.

"There now, I feel more presentable," said the short fat man who re-entered. He'd thrown a tacky flannel bathrobe over the wrinkled candy-stripe pajamas he'd opened the door of his apartment in. His feathery white hair still stood up as though charged with electricity. This was Dr. Oscar Taverner, one of the two

Atlantis scholars they wanted to question. "Can I offer you gentlemen a cup of coffee? Not real coffee, you understand, but a quite adequate wartime substitute a colleague of mine at the university has concocted out of soy beans and dried figs. He's still working on a sugar substitute, so I have to offer it black."

"No thanks, Dr. Taverner," said Smitty.

"Shoo," said the fat white-haired man. A fuzzy black cat went scurrying across his path, leaped up onto a coffee table strewn with thick open books.

"It's very nice of you, doctor, to see us on such short notice," said MacMurdie. He doubted the professor could make it all the way over to his desk without knocking over either a pile of something or a nesting cat.

Taverner succeeded, however, and sank into the swivel chair. He rose again, tugged several back issues of the *New York Times* out from under him and sat again. "I never miss an opportunity, gentlemen, to talk about my hobby horse," he said, wheezing faintly. "Once you announced your wish to discuss the fabled sunken world of Atlantis I was compelled to invite you in."

"What we'd like to know," said Mac, "is whether anyone else has tried to contact you in the past few days in regard to Atlantis."

"You're Mr. Smith, aren't you?"

"No, I'm MacMurdie. This is Mr. Smith sitting next to me."

"You wouldn't have any relatives named Mac-

Quarrie, would you?" asked the professor. "You look very much like one of my former classmates at Heidelberg. We always called him Mac."

"Afraid not, professor." Mac removed a photostat copy of the man from Atlantis story from his pocket. "Did you by any chance notice this story in yesterday's paper? 'Twas only in the early edition."

Taverner's elbow nearly tipped over a stack of scholarly journals as he reached for the clipping. "I'm afraid I'm several days behind in my newspaper reading," he said. "Frankly, I find much of the war news depressing. I remember Europe as it was ten or fifteen years ago and . . . but you came to talk of Atlantis." He began patting the few clear places on his desk top with one open palm. "Aha, here they are. Sometimes the cats take them away, they like to chew on the frames." He put on a lopsided pair of hornrim spectacles.

Smitty felt something dig into his leg. It was a tiny orange kitten using him as a scratching post. "Hello, fellow." He picked up the tiny kitten in one huge hand, lifted it up to his eye level.

"This is quite an interesting item." Taverner removed his spectacles, dropped the photostat among the paper debris that covered his desk. "Fascinating. Of course, there are a good many quacks and charlatans working in the Atlantis field, alas. Still and all, gentlemen, I'd venture to say that the medallion this unfortunate verdant fellow was in possession of sounds like an authentic artifact from long lost Atlantis."

Nodding, Mac asked, "Did this lad try to contact you in any way?"

"Alas, no," said Dr. Taverner. "What makes you ask?"

"We figure he was maybe heading to show some authority on Atlantis that dingus," said Smitty. "You're one of the top guys in the Atlantis business."

"Aha, and so you thought perhaps he had made an appointment with me which his unfortunate public collapse prevented him from keeping."

"That's about it," said MacMurdie. "We were hoping to get a name to hang on the lad."

"Yes, I see. The account did mention he carried no personal identification. Alas, I am afraid no one has offered me a look at anything this potentially interesting in several years. Would that they had." He leaned back, resting his hands on his ample stomach. "Why, may I ask, are you so anxious to learn this man's name? Is it because of your interest in Atlantis, gentlemen?"

"It's more an interest in this particular guy." Smitty gently set the kitten onto a clear stretch of Oriental carpet.

"Is there anything else about the storied continent I can tell you?"

"Not at the moment." Mac rose to his feet, held out his hand to the seated professor. "We thank ye for your time." He shook hands, then retrieved his copy of the newspaper story.

"I always enjoy a chance to ride my hobby horse, gentlemen, though I'm afraid this has been but a short canter." He sighed, easing up to show them out.

Mac and Smitty went down to their car and drove across Manhattan to check on the other name on their list.

Professor Newgrass was not cordial.

He received them in the foyer of his Eastside apartment, a stark eggshell-white room containing two black-framed mirrors, a small circular black table and no chairs.

"I'm afraid my secretary misunderstood you over the phone," he told MacMurdie. He was a tall spare man of fifty-one, wearing a British-cut tweed jacket. "I really don't have time to talk to you now. Who exactly do you claim to represent?"

"'Tis more than a claim," Mac told him. "We work for Justice, Inc."

"My, how noble sounding."

MacMurdie kept his temper and persisted. "It's in reference to this story."

Newgrass ignored the photostat. "I really have no more time I'm afraid." He turned his back, moved toward the inner door. "You apparently told my secretary you had some artifact pertaining to Atlantis to—"

"Whoa now." Smitty had taken three giant

steps and dropped a big hand on the professor's tweedy shoulder.

Newgrass pulled free, faced the big man with an angry frown on his face. "I don't like to be manhandled," he said in a harsh voice. "Now I really must ask you to leave."

"All we want to know is did a guy have an appointment with you, to show you a medallion."

"My affairs are no concern of yours," said the angry Newgrass. "If my secretary hadn't been misinformed by you, you wouldn't have gotten this far. Now, good-bye." He left them.

"What do you think?" said Smitty, looking from the door the professor had used to the Scot.

"I'm thinking," replied MacMurdie, "that I'm glad my days of schooling are behind me. I wouldna care to be taught by that skurlie. Let's go."

In their car again, with Mac at the wheel, Smitty said, "That takes care of our Atlantis experts. We sure didn't learn much."

"If they was telling the truth," said Mac, "we at least know where our green laddie *wasn't* going."

Smitty chuckled. "That only leaves about six or seven million places where he might have been heading."

"Dick suggested we join him in Westchester when we finished our duties here," said Mac. "So let's be off to the one-horse town of Wollterville."

But they never reached their destination.

Boom!

A half hour out of the city, on a quiet country road which wound through grassy fields, there was suddenly a tremendous noise beneath the hood of the automobile.

The hood rose up, detached from the car by the force of the explosion. It flapped through the midday air like a huge monstrous wing.

Thick black smoke came spewing out of the engine. The car went spinning off the road.

CHAPTER X

It's So Peaceful in the Country

There was nothing around but fenced in fields and, in the distance, cows. The truck had pulled up near a huge complex of red barns. About a hundred yards from the barns was a sprawling one story farmhouse. The one-eyed man climbed into the back of the truck, picked up Lizbeth and dropped to the ground with her. The former gorilla hefted Cole Wilson.

"You're a Charles Atlas graduate, no doubt," remarked Cole as he was dumped on the dirt.

"We're going to untie your legs so you can walk," the one-eyed man told him. "You'll notice there's no place much to run to anyway."

"You try to run or anything and I'll drop you," added the man with the .45 automatic.

"Very bucolic," said Cole when he was on his

feet again. One of the slant-roof red barns was filled with milking stalls. Painted on the side of this barn were the words Herky's Dairy in large, faded white letters. "A dairy farm."

"That's exactly where we want you to trot now," ordered the one-eyed man, "into the milking barn."

There was a skinny freckled man of sixty standing in the shadows of the big barn, one sharp elbow resting on a stanchion. He wiped his mouth with the back of a knobby hand, dropping something away in the bib pocket of his overalls. "Hope this ain't going to interfere with my milking," he said.

"Your sense of priorities is snafued, Herky," said the one-eyed man.

"Got to milk them cows ever' afternoon, Broome," said Herky. Up close he smelled strongly of manure and bourbon.

The one-eyed man obviously didn't like the open use of his name. He walked, tight lipped, by the old dairyman. On the wooden barn wall a scythe hung on a wooden peg. Broome caught hold of the scythe, tugged down.

"Come on over here." The gorilla man pointed toward a section of flooring which had just slid aside to reveal a lighted stone stairway leading down underground.

"I hope none of your cows fall through our roof, Mr. Herky," said Cole as he was nudged toward the stairwell by the barrel of the automatic.

At the bottom of the stairs were three doors.

Broome came hurrying down, reached and opened the door on the right. "Go on in."

This was a large room, with walls of knotty pine and black leatherette furniture.

"This is the nicest air raid shelter I've ever been in," said Cole.

Lizbeth was anxiously turning her head from side to side. "I don't . . . my father isn't here."

"We never said he was." Broome stepped out, leaving Cole and the girl locked in the underground room.

The little country railroad station had a peaked black shingle roof and was painted a rusty wine color. Two crates of chickens were sitting on the platform producing protesting clucks. A nine-year-old boy in short pants was bent over a crack in the wood platform, poking a thin wire down. He looked back over his shoulder as Dick Benson and Josh appeared. "You know anything about fishing for money?"

"I used to be pretty good at that," said Josh. Been a long time since I've done anything in that line, though."

"Lost my dime down there, an old time real silver one."

"What you got on the end of that wire, gum?"

"Yeah, and it's my last hunk of gum, too. They run out of gum at Malley's General Store, too."

Josh squatted beside the boy. "Let me get a look down there."

74

Benson, his face expressionless, continued on to the station master's office.

The station master was an enormously fat man of forty. He was wearing, for some reason, a gray sweatsuit and sneakers with his regulation station master's cap. "Howdy do," he said, wiping his sweating face with a blue polka dot bandana. "Help you any? My name's Bud Arnold."

"How many taxis serve this station?" asked the Avenger.

Arnold pushed back from his rolltop desk. "You're maybe wondering why I'm decked out like this," he said.

Benson had no interest in the matter, but for diplomacy's sake he said, "I was rather curious, yes."

"Trying to get in shape," explained the perspiring station master. "I run a mile a day. I'm several pounds overweight. Figure if I get in good shape they'll take me in the Marine Corps. That's just about the only way I'm ever going to get out of Wollterville. Taxis you say?"

"I'd like to talk to all the drivers who bring passengers to this station."

"Now that ain't going to be very hard, mister," said Arnold. "What with gas rationing and the boys who ain't farming or working at the tool and die getting themselves drafted, well, about the only steady taxi we got left is Boggs's."

"Where can I find Boggs?"

"Oh, Boggs don't drive it, he just owns it. See, Boggs the young one, he's in the Army Air Corps

75

and the old man is looking after his mother's place. Fritch is the one you want. Fritch has got bad eyes so they won't take him." He glanced up at the Regulator clock on his office wall. "Won't be another train stopping for an hour and ten minutes. Fritch is more than likely hanging round Malley's store across the street on East Main."

"Thank you," said Benson. "Now I'd like to ask you something else." He described the man from Atlantis, basing his description on the brief look he'd had in the hospital when the man was murdered. "Did you notice him yesterday afternoon?"

"Nope, he don't sound familiar to me," replied Arnold. "Now yesterday afternoon was when that darn crate of pigeons bust out on the platform, so I wasn't paying as close attention as I might usually."

"He doesn't sound like anyone who uses your station regularly?"

"Nope. Can't say as how he does," said the fat man. "You a government agent or a detective or something like that?"

"Something like that." Benson left the man.

"Got the dime," said Josh when the Avenger reappeared on the platform.

"And an extra two bit piece besides," said the elated boy.

"Across the street," Benson said to Josh. "We've got someone to talk to."

"Thanks, mister," the boy called.

Josh waved a good-bye, then asked Benson,

"How many taxi drivers do we have to talk to?"

"Apparently Wollterville has only one regularly operating taxi," answered Benson.

"Middle of nowhere," said the squinting young man. He was standing in the middle of the general store, hands held out toward the squat black-iron stove.

"You didn't pick him up at a house?" asked Benson.

"Nope, out on the road," answered Fritch. "See, he just called me up on the telephone here. Told me to drive three miles out on the old Branchville Road and he'd be there and he was."

"What's near there?"

"Nothing much," said Fritch.

"Say now," said the storekeeper, who'd been leaning on his counter and listening. "Maybe that stranger could of come from Herky's dairy farm."

Fritch scratched his head with a warmed hand. "What makes you think that?"

"Well sir, my delivery boy, old Wally Anderson, said he saw a couple strangers round there when he drove by in the truck last week," said the storekeeper. "Besides, as I calculate, that place where you picked the fellow up is right down behind Herky's place. All a fellow'd have to do is come down through the back pasture."

77

"Never thought of that," said young Fritch. "You might try Herky's dairy, mister."

"We will," said the Avenger.

CHAPTER XI

The Green Man Comes Home

Three bluejays danced on the dry grass nearby, screeching and squawking.

"Why do you no fly South for the winter and leave a mon to die in peace?"

"Hey," said Smitty at some distance.

MacMurdie opened his eyes. He was sprawled on his back in the grass about ten feet up from the edge of the road. "Let me see now," he said in a weak voice, "to the best of my recollection I took a great leap out of the driver's seat when the car blew up."

"You okay over there, Mac?" called Smitty.

"I'm nae sure." MacMurdie decided he would try to move a little. "There feels to be little or nothing broken. Perhaps I'll venture to sit up." This caused the sandy-haired Scot to groan.

"You got a big goose egg on your head." Clothes frayed and dirt-stained, Smitty hobbled over to stand beside his friend.

Locating the bump just above his right ear, Mac gingerly poked at it. "Ow," he said.

Extending a hand, Smitty helped him up. "You're not bleeding much, Mac, except for your nose a little."

MacMurdie tugged out his handkerchief and wiped at his nose. "And what about yourself?"

"Twisted my ankle a little, nothing serious."

MacMurdie surveyed the countryside. "Ah, there sits our devilish machine yonder."

The auto had continued on several hundred feet after the two men had leaped from each side of it. Then it had smashed into a thick roadside oak tree. Smoke was spewing up from the wreck, spurts of flame.

"Somebody planted a bomb on us, huh?" said Smitty, his eyes on the smoking ruin of their car.

"Aye. We should have been on the lookout for that sort of thing."

"Why? Far as we knew the only people who don't want us to investigate this man from Atlantis mess are the FBI and that hush-hush Washington outfit Dick ran up against," said the giant man. "They're not likely to have done something like this."

"No, 'twas done by someone else," agreed Mac. "They had to do it after we left the garage on Bleek Street, while we were doing our questioning."

"That Professor Newgrass guy would have

liked to blow us sky high," said Smitty. "He could have sent his secretary out the back way while we were getting the bum's rush in the foyer."

"That might be. Though maybe it was them skurlies Cole and I tangled with last night."

"But I thought they took off with Cole and the Kearny dame."

"Let's see if we can take a look at the car," suggested Mac, starting down toward the road.

"Yeah, we can maybe . . ." Smitty suddenly stopped, knocking MacMurdie to the ground and diving down beside him. "Gas tank."

The flames had reached the tank. With a huge whomping sound their car climbed into the air, spun and landed with a great smash. Fire crackled over its entire body, blackening it, eating at the paint.

"Darn," said Smitty, "and we had nearly a half tank of gas, too."

Broome crossed to the small stove to pick up the gurgling coffee pot. After filling a mug he returned to the black sofa chair he'd been reclining in. "You've got nothing really to complain about," he said. "I wish I could spend all my time in the country, instead of having to serve in New York City so much."

Three other men were in the underground room with the one-eyed man. The man Broome was addressing himself to was young and fat, a pasty-faced man named Kassock. "I don't call this exactly country life, Broome," he said in his high piping voice. "Living down here most of the time, I feel like I'm holed up in an old subway tunnel."

One of the others, an older man, bald and small, said, "This doesn't strike me as proper talk for two loyal members of the Brotherhood." He gave a crackling laugh, to indicate he was joking with them.

Broome sipped his coffee, saying nothing.

"I'm as loyal as any of you," said fat Kassock. "When we succeed in taking over, I'll work harder than most of you. This waiting around, though, cooped up . . . it's wearying."

The remaining man in the group was thin and pale, wearing a ten-year-old dark blue suit and sitting very straight in a wooden farmhouse chair. "We shouldn't be kidding about the Brotherhood," he said now. "The Brotherhood of the Millennium means a good deal to me. I mean, it's the most important thing in my life."

"*Your* life maybe, Creech," said the fat man. "You're happy just sitting around. But I'm getting a little bored cooped up under a drunken old farmer's barn."

"Glanz didn't like sitting around either," said the small bald man. "They gave him a nice outside job, going into Manhattan to show that medallion to M15. You should have volunteered for a job like that." He gave another cackling laugh.

"You have a repulsive way of laughing," said the fat man.

"Glanz did what he was told," said Creech, "did his duty. We all swore to die for the Brotherhood, you know."

"There's dying and there's dying," said Kassock. "I don't want to end up dying from some crazy germ."

Broome started to say something, then stopped himself. None of the others here knew how the green man had really died.

"You should be happy then," said the bald man to Kassock, "that dear Dr. Kearny is no longer being held here. Now that he and his equipment are far away there's no chance of your coming down with anything."

"That old coot did it deliberately," said Kassock. "He slipped something to Glanz."

The bald man shrugged. "That's the fortunes of war."

"They'll keep a better lookout on the doctor where he is now," said Broome. He finished his coffee, stood up and took the cup to a small sink. "As for your problem, Kassock, I can assure you we'll all be leaving this particular outpost quite soon."

"We should have left a long time ago," said the fat man, rubbing his fingers across a splotched cheek. "They might be able to backtrack on Glanz, find out he came from this place."

"They haven't yet," said Broome. "Neither the FBI nor any other agency knows where their green man came from."

"You sure of that?" asked the bald man.

Broome nodded his head. "Still it's been decided that eventually they may get a lead to friend Herky's. So we'll be moving out, with our prisoners, after nightfall."

"Herky," said Kassock. "He's liable to talk."

"He won't be in any condition to talk when we take our leave."

"Nothing must stand in the way of the Brotherhood," said the bald man.

Creech turned toward him. "I don't like your remarks. They smack of disloyalty to me."

"You've got cabin fever, Creech," the small man told him. "Everything gets on your nerves. You and the baby blimp ought to take a walk."

"A person can't help being fat," said Kassock. "It all has to do with—"

A faintly sounding buzzer interrupted him. Broome went to an intercom phone next to the stove. "Yes, what is it?"

"He's back," said the voice from above.

"Who, who's back?"

"Glanz," came the answer.

CHAPTER XII

The Brotherhood of the Millennium

It was cold in Vermont. A harsh wind came slashing through the twisted leafless trees which surrounded the isolated lodge. The wind sighed around the big many-roomed lodge, worrying at the brown wood shingles.

The chill ground crackled and gravel scattered as a car approached the house. There was a lone man in the car. He parked a few yards from the closed garages at the rear of the lodge. As he got out of the machine he turned up the collar of his black overcoat.

Several of the lodge windows were masked by shutters. The rest had heavy drapes drawn over them.

The man in the black overcoat, one hand holding his coat collar up and the other jammed

85

down tight in his pocket, walked up three of the six wide wooden steps that led to the front door. He stopped, eyes on the heavy oaken door above him.

A moment passed. Then the door swung inward.

The man in the black overcoat climbed the remainder of steps, went inside. When he was in the shadowy hallway the heavy door shut behind him.

"You keep this place much too hot," he said, struggling out of his overcoat.

The man who'd opened and closed the door was small, not more than five feet tall. He was in his early thirties and the thick red hair that covered his head was obviously false. "Don't blame me." He caught the other man's overcoat, nodding at a point down the hall. "Take it up with him, Slaw."

Slaw said, "You'll all end up with respiratory complaints." He went along the hall, went into the second door on the left. There was a sofa drawn up to within three feet of the big fireplace. A fire, built of sturdy logs, was burning away.

"Join me by the fire, M103," invited a voice from the sofa.

Slaw remained near the doorway. "It's a wonder you don't melt, Lund."

"A few pounds wouldn't be missed." Lund was a very fat man, weighing over three hundred and fifty pounds. His bulk filled most of the cushion space. "You've been quite successful. Allow me to congratulate you, M103."

"Thank you, M22." Slaw took a few steps toward the very fat man. "What's that smell?"

"I've been toasting marshmallows," answered Lund. "Some of them got a bit burned."

Slaw said, "I got the medallion, as I already reported."

"Yes, that was excellent work," said the very fat man. "You never did give me all the details."

"I took it from Glanz after I killed him."

"They'd allowed him to keep it, eh?"

"Apparently they couldn't pry it from his hand."

"Don't give me any more details on that aspect of things."

Slaw said, "I delivered the medallion to M3."

"Yes, I've had a preliminary report from him already."

"What does he think?"

"The thing is real, and it should yield the key to . . . to what we think it will."

Slaw crossed to a window. The thick drapes hid the late afternoon from him. "I really wonder," he said, "if this is something we should be bothering ourselves with."

"Let me remind you, Slaw, that you are only 103 in the Brotherhood. Let those of us in the upper echelons worry about policy."

"That's what's wrong with the present system of government in this country," said Slaw as he turned to look at the very fat man. "A small group runs everything, in spite of all the talk about democracy."

Lund waved a very fat hand in the air. "Surely you don't think the Brotherhood of the Millennium is planning to initiate some new form of democracy."

"I'm as aware of our ideals and intentions as you are, Lund," he answered. "As I understand the Brotherhood, each of us has a say, each of the elect."

"True, M103, true," said Lund.

"Well, then . . . we want to concentrate on our primary objectives. This war isn't going to last forever. We must move now to gain control of—"

"Patience, Slaw." From somewhere underneath his sprawling bulk Lund produced a paperbag full of marshmallows. He began popping them into his mouth. "You must realize that our cause will be aided considerably if we can acquire the . . . the cash value of what we're looking for."

"Perhaps, but—"

"There's really no need to debate," the very fat man said as he chewed. "A decision has already been made."

"All we seem to be doing is losing time. Entrusting the medallion to a fool like Glanz was a bad mistake. I told you all at the time—"

"Glanz was a bit careless, agreed. He's more than paid for his folly."

"A bit careless? Lord, he allowed Kearny to inject him with something. He fell down in the middle of a busy New York street, babbling out all our secrets." Slaw slapped a fist into his palm. "It's a wonder he didn't tell all about the Brotherhood."

"But Glanz didn't spill anything that important. We *know* that," said Lund. "Granted we all made a mistake in regard to the good doctor. We assumed the docility drug we gave him was strong enough to keep him under control. Different people react in different ways to different drugs. Obviously Dr. Kearny merely feigned cooperation." He paused to swallow. "Now that we have him working here there's very little risk of any further unfortunate incidents."

"Glanz must have told him what he was going to do," said Slaw. "That's why Kearny gave him ... whatever it was he gave him. He knew Glanz would collapse in Manhattan and—"

"Glanz had an unfortunate habit of taunting people. When he was guarding Kearny he must have told him about what we were planning to do with the medallion. The doctor saw a chance to get a message to the outside world. When he gave Glanz some slow-working drug—perhaps one of the germs he's been working with—he knew that Glanz would probably collapse in some public place with that medallion on him."

"A nasty way of doing it," said Slaw. "He knew what he was slipping to Glanz might kill him."

Lund laughed, a sputtering laugh which sprayed powdered sugar. "No nastier than slitting Glanz's throat for him."

"That was done for the good of the Brotherhood," said Slaw.

Off in the corner the phone rang. "Answer that, will you?"

Slaw caught up the receiver. "Hello?" he said. "Yes, sir. Just a moment. It's M3 for you."

"Hand me the phone."

"It won't reach that far."

"Yes, it will. If you stretch the cords as far as you can."

"Why you simply don't . . ." Slaw sighed, got the phone into his superior's hand. He parted the drapes an inch and looked out.

The man on the other end of the phone was many hundreds of miles away. The first thing he said to Lund was, "By now, at least two of the Avenger's lackeys should be dead."

Lund rubbed the fingers of his free hand together, causing powdered sugar to flicker through the air. "How did you manage that, M3?"

"A simple matter," replied M3. "An explosive device attached to their car, timed to explode when they were far, far from my doorstep. I must make a note to listen to the radio later on and see if the announcement of their untimely end makes the news."

"Nothing but war news these days."

"There's something even more important to

tell you. I have translated the inscription on the medallion. It does indeed give the specifics we anticipated."

"A location, you mean?"

"Exactly," replied M3, with a chuckle. "I have conveyed this interesting information to M1 himself. He, in turn, has asked me to pass on some preliminary instructions to you."

"Yes, go ahead."

"You are to prepare your guest for a trip. A trip out of the country."

"Can arrangements for such a trip be made?" asked Lund. "How can we get out of—"

"It will all be taken care of. All you have to do is prepare Kearny, Lund, and make sure you leave no traces of his work behind. Is that quite clear?"

"Yes, no traces."

"Unfortunately, prior commitments make it impossible for me to accompany you," continued M3. "A pity, since I haven't been to . . . to the islands in question for many, many years. You'll make your preparations now. Further instructions will be coming to you within an hour."

Lund began the slow process of getting himself up off the sofa. "I'll start at once."

"Bon voyage," said M3 and broke the connection.

"You can put the phone back," the very fat man told Slaw.

While Slaw was carrying the receiver over to hang it up he asked, "What did M3 say?"

"We're all going on a trip."

"Where?"

"To Atlantis," replied the very fat man.

CHAPTER XIII

"You're Supposed To Be Dead!"

Old Wally Anderson was a great admirer of the Andrews Sisters. At home, in the room he rented at the back of Malley's General Store, he had quite a stack of their records. He was humming his version of their latest hit now as he guided the rattletrap delivery truck over the roads and lanes of Wollterville.

"What could have happened to them fellers?" he exclaimed to himself when he noticed the two bedraggled men standing at the side of the road up ahead in the afternoon light.

Wally slowed. You had to go easy with the brakes or the truck would buck like a wild horse in the movies. He gradually depressed the brake pedal, bringing the truck to a clattering halt a few feet from MacMurdie and Smitty. "You fellows run out of gas?"

"We ran out of car," replied MacMurdie.

"How's that again?"

"We had a little accident," said Smitty, jerking his blackened thumb in the direction of the ruin of their vehicle.

Wally adjusted his rimless bifocals and leaned toward the windshield. "By golly, I'm darned if you didn't," he said when he spotted what was left of the exploded automobile. "How'd you come to bust her up so good?"

Mac and Smitty had just been going over the machine and its now scattered parts. They'd found a few remnants of the time device bomb used. This intelligence they kept to themselves.

"Must have been that bootleg gasoline we were using," said Mac.

The old delivery boy nodded understandingly. "Old man Hodgins over in Abeltown tried something like that," he said. "Got himself convinced you could run a car on applejack, which he happened to have a lot of handy. As it turned out, the engine went darned good on hard cider. Only problem was, it didn't stay in the car. Shot clean through the hood and . . . can I give you a lift anywheres?"

"We'd sure appreciate," said Smitty, "a ride into Wollterville."

"Well sir, I can sure enough do that," said Wally. "Got a couple more deliveries to take care of first, though. Hop in, the both of you. Don't worry about getting dirt and gunk on this upholstery 'cause it's beyond fretting over."

When they were bouncing along, Mac asked, "You lived around here most of your life?"

"Well, I grew up over in Abeltown. Only been living in Wollterville about twenty-seven, twenty-eight years."

"Ye probably know most everyone herrreabouts."

"Sure, and they know me," answered Wally.

"Many new people moving into this area these days?" asked Smitty. He was sitting next to the door, his elbow stuck out the window.

"Nope," answered the old man. "This is more a town people move away from. Young people, I mean, they simply don't seem satisfied with the quiet kind of life we got. 'Course the Army takes a good many of them, too."

"So there aren't many strangers around then?" Mac inquired.

"You two fellers are the first I've seen in a couple of weeks or more."

MacMurdie scratched at his ribs with his smudged hand. "You saw some other out-oftowners back a couple weeks ago?"

"Well sir, might be they was merely some out-of-town kin of Herky's," said Wally. "They sure didn't look like they was related to him, one being short and dark and the other thin and fair. 'Course my Aunt Cordelia had twin boys and one of them was—"

"Who's Herky?" cut in Smitty.

"Owns Herky's Dairy."

95

"Maybe the guys you saw were just customers."

"Nope, they was out-of-town fellers, suit and necktie sort of fellers."

"Whereat is this farm?" asked Mac.

"Oh, 'bout six seven miles up this road as we're on now and then two miles right on Bayberry Road."

"I havena seen a dairy farm since I was a wee bairn," said Mac. "'Twould be a joy to wander around one again. Do ye think you can drop us off near there?"

"Take you right up to the door if you want," offered the old man. "It's milking time, though, and Herky probably won't have much time to show you around."

"You don't have to drive us all the way there," said Smitty. "We like hiking, especially through such pleasant countryside."

"Well then I'll drop you off at Bayberry Road." The old man ran his tongue over the front teeth of his dental plate a few times. "Ain't you anxious to have something done about your car?"

"'Tis beyond help I fear," Mac told him. "Though we will be coming in and making a report to your local police about it."

"Hard to buy a good used car these days," said Wally. "I'm waiting for them new cars they're going to be coming out with when this war's over. I bet they're going to be something. I want to get me one that's really streamlined."

Fifteen minutes later they reached Bayberry Road. Mac and Smitty jumped down.

Broome, alone, shoved open the door of the farmhouse. The lookout man who'd phoned down to him was standing in front of a lopsided spinning wheel holding a cup of cold coffee.

A man who appeared to be Glanz sat in a chintz covered chair, hands, one bandaged, folded in his lap. There was a green tint to his face, a gauze bandage round his neck.

"You're supposed to be dead," said Broome.

"Everybody'd like that," came the raspy, hoarse reply. "But I want my share of things."

"What's wrong with your voice?"

A horrible dry laugh came out of the man. "Having your throat slashed doesn't do your vocal cords much good."

"Why'd you come back here?"

"Where else could I go?"

"We moved the doctor up to Lund's." Broome moved closer to the seated man. "We're all getting out of here."

"And left me for dead."

"That wasn't my idea," said Broome. "It came from higher up in the Brotherhood." He stopped beside a round lamp table, staring at the man who looked like Glanz. The late afternoon sunlight slanting in at the window just missed touching the man.

The Avenger met his gaze. He was aware his impersonation of the dead man was far from perfect. He'd only seen the man for a few minutes in the Westlake Hospital. In order to bring off this imitation Benson had again used the drug which, when injected into the flesh of his face, made it as pliable as modeling clay. To duplicate the color of the man from Atlantis's eyes he'd use tinted little contact lenses which fit over his eyeballs. The extra height needed was supplied by built-up shoes. Benson knew he was a reasonable facsimile of the dead man, but there were a good many fine details about him he couldn't even guess at. He had no idea what Glanz's voice had been like. Until he'd walked up to the farm house and the nervous lookout man had run out and blurted, "Glanz!" the Avenger hadn't even known the name of the man he was pretending to be.

The Avenger was aware of the serious chance he was taking, but the taking of great risks had become a habit with him. A habit it was impossible to break.

"It really nearly floored me when I saw him come walking up to the front door big as life," said the lookout man. He was a middle-sized chunky man. "It really gave me—"

"You shouldn't have come here like this," Broome said.

"Too many people were interested in me in New York City," croaked the Avenger. "They wanted to talk to me about a lot of things I didn't care to talk about. See, I'm still loyal to the Brotherhood."

"I don't know what we're going to do with you."

"You better not try to knock me off again."

"I told you, Glanz, I didn't give that order."

There's nothing to worry about," said Benson. "When you guys move out I'll go, too."

"That I can't say yes or no to." Broome paced around the room. He stopped by the lookout man. "Is there any more coffee out in Herky's kitchen?"

"Yeah, he's always got a pot on the stove. I think he's hoarding a few sacks of coffee beans someplace."

"Get me a cup."

"When you pulling out?" the Avenger asked.

"Maybe tonight," answered Broome.

"What about the girl? She still here?"

"Yeah, her and that jerk who works with Justice, Inc."

"You haven't knocked him off yet?"

"He's going to be questioned when we get to Lund's."

The lookout man came in carrying three cups of hot coffee. "Thought you might like . . ." He tripped on a wrinkle in the rug. All three cups left his hands to go spinning through the air.

Burning coffee splashed across Benson's face, splattering at his neck. He jumped up and back.

"Gee, I'm sorry," said the lookout man. "And I got your bandage all spoiled."

Before Benson could stop him the chunky man trotted over to him and began to dab at the Avenger's neck with his handkerchief. "There's no need to—"

"Hey!" The lookout man backed off.

"What is it?" asked Broome.

"There's no cut under those bandages."

A .38 revolver appeared in Broome's hand. "Get the rest of the men up here," he said to the lookout man. "I think we've caught ourselves another fish."

CHAPTER XIV

Getaway

With his back against the door of the underground room in which they were imprisoned Cole Wilson looked up at the ceiling. "The cows are coming home," he observed.

The lowing and mooing of the milk cows, the clang of a cowbell, came down dimly from above.

Lizbeth was sitting, arms folded and knees tight together, on the leatherette sofa. She said nothing.

Cole, grinning, walked over and sat down beside her. "They should provide sufficient noise for my purposes."

Her left eyebrow flickered. "What do you have in mind?"

"You must realize by now, dear girl, that your

101

father is not being held here." He spoke low and close to her ear. "He may have been here, but no more. Furthermore, it's possible they don't intend to take you to him at all."

"Then why have they kidnapped me?"

"Maybe to find out what you're up to . . . or to keep you from consulting the Avenger," said Cole. "And even if they are going to arrange a reunion . . . it doesn't include me. Me, the last of the Wilsons, they may just leave in a hole in the ground in one of these country fields."

"They wouldn't—"

"Look, I can get us out of here."

"No, I don't—"

"Yes, we've been over that. But I'm trying to tell you the chance of being taken to your father by these boys is a fifty-fifty one at best," Cole told her. "We can find your father a lot faster when we're free."

"Why do you say that?"

"Because we'll be working with everybody in Justice, Inc."

One of the cows up above gave an annoyed moan, hooves stomped on the barn floor.

"All right," said the redhaired girl. "I have to admit my approach isn't getting me anywhere. And there's your future to think about, too. What are you going to do?"

Patting her on the shoulder, Cole stood up. "I've cased this room pretty thoroughly. There's no evidence they have any way of watching us. There also don't seem to be any hidden microphones." He sauntered over to the door. "With the bovine chorus going on upstairs I don't think anyone'll notice a bit of tinkering on my part."

Cole extracted a small silver tool from the cuff of his trousers. He squatted in front of the lock mechanism, concentrating on picking it.

"Suppose some kind of alarm goes off when the door's opened?"

"Then you'll be able to tell your grandchildren you once saw Cole Wilson blush." He worked deftly on the lock.

In roughly two and a half minutes there came a satisfying click.

Cole, slowly and carefully, turned the door knob. "No bells so far." He beckoned the girl to join him.

"Be careful," she said. "Don't get yourself hurt."

He grinned at her. "It's refreshing to see you've had a change of heart, Lizbeth." He began to push very gradually against the door.

When it had opened an inch outward Cole stopped and listened. Nearly thirty seconds passed before he started pushing again. "You wait here till I come fetch you."

He eased himself through the ten-inch opening.

Lizbeth waited, breath held.

"Say—!" said a voice that was not Cole's.

The girl brought one hand up to her face. She stayed exactly where she was, not knowing what had happened out in the corridor and afraid to look.

Then a hand reached in and caught hold of her arm.

"Come along, angel," said Cole.

He pulled her out of their prison room, led her down the corridor toward the stairs.

A man in a tan suit was spreadeagled on the floor, flat on his face and unconscious. Lizbeth had never seen him before.

"Step over the gentleman who was on guard duty," whispered Cole. He hurried Lizbeth up the stone stairs to the trap door. "Now let us hope there is some kind of doodad that opens this door from our side."

There was.

"I'm wondering," said MacMurdie as he and Smitty cut across a field of dry grass, "how 'twould be to retire in some idyllic spot like this here."

"Quiet," said Smitty.

"I fear so," agreed Mac. "And once the love of fighting and hunting down skurlies gets hold of a mon ... 'tis no use to contemplate the quiet life."

Suddenly a few feet in front of them a frightened pheasant came whirring up out of the high grass.

"Whoosh," said Mac.

"Hold it," said Smitty, "let's get down." He threw himself out flat on the grass.

"You hear something besides that great flapping bird?" whispered Mac, stretched out next to the giant.

"Yeah, up above us someplace," replied Smitty.

"Well sir, let's work ourrr way up there and have a look."

"You notice the grove of apple trees at the crest of the hill? I think I heard somebody say something up there."

"I nae heard a word."

"Maybe I'm wrong," admitted Smitty. "But it's also possible these guys, if this is one of their hideouts, got some men posted a little ways off from the place itself."

"Aye, 'tis highly possible."

The two men had the ability to crawl through the high grass silently, moving it no more than the gentle wind which was blowing across the field.

After they'd traveled over a hundred yards flat out on their stomachs, Smitty reached out and touched his companion's arm. He inclined his head to their right.

"You got to get more sleep," someone was saying in among the trees.

"I heard something," said a raspy voice. "Something besides that stupid bird I mean."

"Put that rod away. You go shooting quail and the game warden or some other rube's going to run us in."

"That wasn't no quail. A quail is a little fat thing, with its feathers sticking all up like that. What that bird was, it was a grouse."

"You don't know any more about birds than

I do. It sure looked like all the pictures of quail I've seen."

"Actually, mon," said MacMurdie as he appeared to them from behind a tree trunk with a revolver dangling casually in his hand, "'twas a pheasant."

The man with his gun out was a thickset fellow in a dark pinstripe suit. He decided he could shoot Mac before the Scot could raise his revolver.

He was wrong. He got the shot off but it came nowhere near MacMurdie. And before he could try again Mac had put a slug in his gun arm a little below the elbow.

Josh was hunched in the front seat of the car. "Let's see now," he was murmuring to himself, eyes half closed, "how would Josh Elijah H. Newton, Jr. sound? No, I don't think I want him to be junior. People named junior never get anyplace in the world. Although I suppose Horatio Alger, Jr. did okay. At least, he was famous in his day. How would that sound? Horatio Alger Newton. No, they'd laugh at that. Kids got a way, nice as they are sometimes, of laughing at you for a name like that." He changed his position, crossed his legs a new way. "Best thing is going to be a nice simple name. Now maybe Rosabel isn't going to sit still for that. Bob, that's a nice simple name. Nobody laughs at you if your name is Bob. Well, they laugh at Bob Hope but that just means money in his pocket. Robert J. Newton, that's pretty good. J. for Josh, of course. That way it kind of ties him in with me, but not so strong as if we was to name him straight out junior."

Sitting up straight, Josh looked out the window. They had parked their vehicle a safe distance from the dairy farm. Benson had told Josh to wait here for at least an hour before coming after him.

"Hour's near about up," Josh decided. "Maybe I ought to go scout around that place." He rubbed a hand across his chin. "No, better give Dick the full hour. He can handle himself."

He slouched again. "How would that sound. Richard Henry Newton? No, I think Bob's better. But what was that name Rosabel wanted to stick on him? After some movie actor. Ronald, wasn't it? That's no name for anybody."

Josh locked his hands around his knee. "Of course, it might turn out to be a girl," he said. "That's what my aunt was telling me in her last letter. Lot of girls born into our family. Yeah, but if it's a girl I can't even think of one name."

He straightened again, put aside all personal thoughts. The hour that the Avenger had told him to wait was running out. Josh had to be ready for action.

The Avenger made a slight bow in the direction of the fat young man in the circle of a half-dozen men that faced him across the farmhouse parlor. "Exactly," he said in his level voice.

Kassock had just said, "I bet you this guy's the Avenger."

The thin pale Creech hurried to one of the windows and pushed aside the curtains. "They might all be out there," he said. "Every single one of those vigilantes of his."

"Are they?" Broome moved the barrel of his pistol to within an inch of Benson's chest.

"You'd be wise to surrender yourselves to me now," said Benson.

"Creech, you and Curly go out the back way," ordered Broome. "Take a real good look around."

"You want everybody we find brought back alive?" asked the small bald Curly.

"We got the kingfish, we don't need the small fry," said the one-eyed Broome. "But don't make any noise when you get rid of them. We don't want the yokels getting curious."

The two men hurried out through the kitchen.

"You're not planning to murder the FBI agents who are out there, too?" Benson asked.

"Quit bluffing." Broome chuckled. "There's not a G-man within a hundred miles of us. If there were, I'd know."

"You have an unusual degree of confidence."

"Maybe that's because—" The one-eyed man didn't get to finish his sentence.

With lightning swiftness the Avenger had made a move.

Instead of trying to get away from Broome, Benson walked right into him. He dodged the man's gun hand. He got a grip on Broome's wrist, forced the gun from his hand at the same time that he spun the man around.

Broome now shielded the Avenger from the remaining men in the room. Before they could draw out their guns he tossed Broome into them.

Again with incredible swiftness he went out the window. Glass exploded out into the afternoon.

The Avenger landed like an acrobat, doubled up and hugging his knees.

He sprinted across the bare ground beside the farmhouse, aimed at the distant road.

He heard more glass smashing behind him. And somewhere a pickup truck was starting its motor.

"You're not going to make it, Avenger!" called Broome. He'd leaped out of the window, too, and was in pursuit. His gun was again in his hand.

The Avenger kept on running.

"I'll drop you in your tracks if you don't stop."

Benson did not stop.

The gun barked once.

The shot missed him.

Then the roar of the truck motor grew very loud. Broome cried out, "What the hell are you doing?"

There was a hollow whumping sound.

The Avenger looked back over his shoulder and saw Broome spinning through the air. The blue pickup truck with Herky's Milk & Butter lettered on its door had sideswiped the one-eyed man.

The truck reversed, bucked some and then swerved to come after the Avenger.

"Give you a lift, Richard Henry?" called Cole Wilson from the driver's seat.

Benson had his special pistol in his hand now. "Swing that truck around," he said. "There are some more of them in there. If they come after me I'd like to bag a couple more of them. Park here and we'll use the truck for a wall."

Cole parked the borrowed truck on the grassy field. "I was rather fancying the idea of using it to make our getaway in," he said. "This spirited redhead beside me is Miss Lizbeth Kearny. Miss Kearny, Richard Henry Benson."

"Duck," said Benson to his aide.

Fat young Kassock had emerged out the front door of the farmhouse with a shotgun. He was hesitating on the porch, watching the performance of the pickup.

"Stop that racket!" Herky came tottering out of the milking barn. "Don't you know any better than to shoot off firearms when cows are being milked?"

"Now look, Mr. Herky—" began Kassock.

Both front windows of the house popped, turning into thousands of bright fragments of glass. Several different kinds of firearms went off inside the house.

"Dang fools," said Herky as he went stalking toward his parlor.

"I'll be much obliged to ye if you'll drop that weapon, skurlie." MacMurdie stepped out onto the porch, carrying two hand guns.

Kassock blinked. He let the shotgun fall at his feet.

Smitty came out into the sunlight now. He had a man under each arm. "Darned if the rest of them didn't get away."

The Avenger circled the hood of the truck, ran to where the stunned Broome was just now struggling to sit up. "We don't want to lose you," he said as he took hold of the man's arm. "I have the feeling you're the kingfish of this bunch here."

"Hi, Dick," called Smitty. "We were just coming down to nose around a little when two fellows tried to shoot us. So we figured we must be at the right place."

"Is that about all the noise you're going to make for today?" asked Herky.

"It's going to be awful quiet around here from now on," MacMurdie told the dairyman.

Benson sensed someone else was approaching. He turned, looking uphill.

Josh was walking down through the waning afternoon. "Looks like I missed the party," he said.

CHAPTER XV

A New Kind of Death

The one-eyed man had no idea where he was.

Broome awakened in a small room. There were no windows, the walls were painted a noncommittal green, and there were three plain wooden chairs against one wall. There didn't seem to be a door.

Getting to his feet, Broome remembered something of what had happened to him. He remembered being flipped by that damn pickup truck of Herky's, remembered being trussed up and dumped in the back of a car. But that was all he did remember. Where he was, how long he'd been there . . . he had no idea.

"You're not the law, Avenger," he called out. "You can't keep me locked up like this."

Broome wasn't even certain, though, if he was still in the hands of Justice, Inc.

"Where else could I be?" he asked himself. "This sure isn't like any jailhouse I've ever heard of."

The hissing sound commenced a few seconds before the one-eyed man noticed it. He'd been walking slowly by the row of three chairs, wondering whether to sit down in one or use it to try to smash through one of the walls.

"What's that?"

Broome looked up toward the green ceiling. There was nothing to see. The hissing continued.

"What are you trying to do to me?" he shouted. "Is that gas you're pouring in here?"

He made an anxious circle of the small room, almost running. He grabbed up a chair by its back.

"I'll break out of here. I'll . . ."

Broome straightened up, placed the chair carefully down on the green floor and sat in it.

Five minutes later a section of the wall slid aside. The Avenger came into the room. Little blond Nellie, holding a notebook and a pencil, followed. The wall closed.

"What's your name?" Benson asked as he took one of the remaining chairs.

Nellie seated herself in the third chair, licked the tip of the pencil, and held it poised over the open page.

Broome was surprised to find himself answering. "My name is Hobart Broome. I don't much like my first name, though."

The one-eyed man didn't know that the invisible gas which had recently filled this room was an invention of Dick Benson, with an assist from MacMurdie. Once he'd breathed a few lungfuls of it he was compelled to tell the truth, to answer every question put to him. The effects wouldn't wear off for over an hour.

"Who are you working for?"

"I don't work for anyone. We're all equal in the Brotherhood."

"What is the Brotherhood?"

"The Brotherhood of the Millennium is an organization devoted to establishing a new and better government in this country.

"By what means?"

"Any means that will succeed in bringing about our goal," answered Broome. "Now, when the whole nation is preoccupied with the war, is a good time to overthrow the established system."

"How many members does your organization have?"

"There are a thousand in the first rank, the elect. Then there are many thousand more who are simply underlings, men who will not have any say in the new system we set up. A system, I might add, that will bring a thousand years of peace and prosperity. A system, which by shedding outmoded and foolish ideas about equality, will—"

"Why was Dr. Kearny taken?"

"We needed him," replied Broome. "The new weapons the government had him working on are absolutely fantastic." He placed his palms on his knees, leaning forward. "There will be no need of guns and bombs. We can kill with the simplest things . . . chemicals, drugs, germs. We can wipe out whole populations if need be, wipe out anyone who stands in the way of the Brotherhood."

"What was Glanz's mission? Why was he sent to New York?"

"Ah, now that was a bonus. When we were first interrogating Kearny, persuading him to work in the lab we'd provided him, we found out what the medallion meant. We'd already had a hint of that from M3."

"What did the medallion mean?"

"Dr. Kearny had just gotten hold of it, but he was pretty certain of what it was," said Broome. "It told where some of the treasure salvaged from Atlantis had been buried, buried centuries ago."

"Isn't that a little out of your line? Treasure hunting."

"We're talking about a treasure worth possibly several million dollars. The Brotherhood needs funds."

"So Glanz was given the medallion to bring to some expert in New York City?"

"He was to take it to M3 for a translation of that scrawling on the back," answered Broome. "That told where the treasure is. Kearny himself wasn't able to translate that."

"But things went wrong."

"Somehow Kearny got close enough to Glanz

to give him a shot of something. He knew Glanz was going to Manhattan that night with the medallion."

"A desperate attempt to send some word of himself to the outside," said the Avenger. "He knew that if Glanz were found suffering from that particular rare disorder and holding the medallion someone would realize that Glanz had come from the place Kearny was being held."

"What Dr. Kearny didn't know was that we never allow men on special missions like Glanz's to carry any identification," said Broome. "So it was a dead end."

"Not exactly," said Benson. "Since we found you as a result. Where is Kearny now?"

"He was moved to Vermont, to a new lab setup there."

"Give me the exact location."

Broome did.

"Now I want some names," said the Avenger.

Nellie flipped to a fresh page in her steno book.

"I want the names," said Benson, "of the top men in your organization."

"I don't know all the names," said Broome. "The two top leaders I know only by number. M1 and M2. I've had no direct contact with them."

"But you know who M3 is," said the Avenger.

Nodding, Broome gave him the name.

"Whoosh," said MacMurdie. "So that's who had that infernal mechanism rigged under our hood."

"Huh," grunted Smitty in surprise. "That just goes to show you can't judge—"

"What about this secret society of theirs?" put in Cole.

The members of Justice, Inc. were all seated around Dick Benson's office. He had just finished telling them about what he'd learned from the truth-drugged Broome. The Avenger was able to give them a concise summary, without having to consult the notes Nellie had taken.

"We had several organizations like this flourishing before the war," replied Benson. "This one seems to have held on."

" 'Tis not like the Bund, though, from the sound of it," said Mac, "nor them various marching lads in their colored shirts."

"No," said the Avenger, "the Brotherhood of the Millennium isn't connected with any of the Axis powers."

"Homegrown crackpots," observed Cole.

"But fairly powerful crackpots," said Nellie, running her fingertips over the cover of her steno book.

"Are they, though?" said Cole. "I know this Broome chap had to tell you the truth. But he wouldn't be the first flunky who was given an exaggerated idea of his organization by the boys higher up."

The Avenger slowly shook his head from side to side once. "I believe the Brotherhood is a dangerous organization," he said. "That's why we have to stop them, to stamp out the whole setup."

"Maybe," suggested Josh, "the reason we been having so much opposition in this investigation is because the Brotherhood has got itself a couple of members in pretty high places."

Cole locked his hands behind his head, grinning. "That's possible," he conceded. "Kind of farfetched, though, isn't it?"

"Mon, there's nothing farfetched about the weapons Kearny was working on," said MacMurdie. "If these Brotherhood skurlies should get hold of some of that stuff . . . well, 'twould nae be too good for the future of this country."

Turning toward Benson, Cole asked, "From what you got out of Broome . . . they don't have anything yet? Any chemical or biological weapon ready to try out."

"No, there's still a little time," answered the Avenger. "What Kearny used on the green man was something still in the experimental stage." He rested his hands on the edge of the desk. "Now, there's still a good deal of work to be done."

"I'll volunteer to go up to Vermont and extricate the professor," offered Cole. "I promised Lizbeth she could tag along."

"No, I have something else for you to do," said Benson. "I want you and Josh to locate the man we now know is M3. Find out what he knows, what he told the organization about the medallion."

Cole shrugged. "Okay," he said. He glanced over at Nellie. "Don't smirk, pixie. My relationship with the fair Miss Kearny is still young. Sooner or later, I'll be spending time with her."

Easing out of his chair, Josh said, "Let's get us a car and start hunting."

"Don't let that skurlie plant any bombs on ye," said Mac as the two men left.

The Avenger pushed himself back from his desk. "Mac, you and I will go on up to Vermont," he said.

"What about me?" asked Smitty.

"You and Nellie stay here," said Benson.

Smitty scratched at his ear. "Maybe I ought to go down to the guest room where Miss Kearny is staying," he said. "And tell her what's up."

"There's no need of that yet," said the Avenger. With a curt nod at Mac, he left the room. MacMurdie followed.

Nellie pursed her lips, frowning at Smitty. "You're as bad as Cole."

CHAPTER XVI

Traps

The chimes in the campus bell tower began to ring. It was ten o'clock, a crisp clear night.

"This reminds me of several of the colleges I was expelled from," said Cole Wilson.

He and Josh were walking along a tree-lined path on the campus of a Westchester County college.

"I didn't have as wide a range to choose from," said the black man. "So I stuck with Tuskegee."

"Oh, there were a couple of places I attended where I would have been happy to continue." Cole was strolling with both hands in the pockets of his trousers. "I enjoyed the three and a half months I spent at UCLA, for instance. And Heidelberg had some interesting extracurricular attractions, but I decided Germany wasn't the place to pursue an education in 1936."

"That's the building we want over there, the English Department." Josh nodded to his left. "The brick setup with all that ivy crawling up it."

"I wonder if there's a special breed of ivy they get for colleges," said Cole as they turned onto another path.

"You still want to walk right in on Taverner?"

"Seems to me the best approach," said Cole. "I'm sure he's still pretending to be the bumbling and lovable old codger he was when Mac and Smitty called on him this morning."

"That wasn't a very lovable thing to do, planting a bomb in their car."

"One of his minions must have done the actual planting."

The Avenger had assigned Cole and Josh to find Dr. Taverner and question him. The two Justice, Inc. teammates had learned that the professor had left his New York City apartment at midday to come out to this campus.

"Taverner is M3," mused Josh. "Who do you think M1 and M2 will turn out to be?"

"Well, if this were a mystery novel by one of those hefty English ladies with the battleship faces I'd say we should look for the least likely suspect."

There were still several lights on in the offices of the three story brick building which housed the English Department. Two coeds in cashmere sweaters, checked skirts and bobby sox were sitting on the stone steps of the building talking, their books hugged tight to their chests.

"Least likely, huh?" said Josh. "Who would that be then?"

Cole had been looking at the two girls, one blond and one brunette. He grinned at them when they turned to look over at him. "College girls are starting to seem very young to me," he said to his black companion. "The least likely suspect in this mess would be . . . probably Dr. Kearny himself."

Josh laughed as he pushed open the glass door. "That's a great notion. He had himself kidnapped, gave that Brotherhood guy a shot of germs, ordered his own daughter grabbed by those heavies . . . all to throw off suspicion."

"Unfortunately life isn't an English detective story," said Cole. "Things aren't as neat and well-ordered. Which office is Dr. Taverner supposed to be inhabiting?"

"203, which should be up on the second floor."

The two men started up a shadowy stairway.

"How's Rosabel, by the way?" asked Cole while they hunted the hallway for the right door.

"Doing fine."

"How far off is it?"

"Little over six months."

Cole halted in front of a frosted glass door. "Here it is. Doesn't look like anyone is home."

The office beyond the door appeared dark. There was a small file card taped to the door.

Josh stooped to read the message written on

the card. "Says here Taverner can be found from 9:30 on at the Men's Gym."

"That's the place for us then," said Cole.

There were three coeds on the front steps when they came out, the new one a redhead. All of them watched Cole.

"Obviously I'm still attractive to college girls," remarked Cole as he and Josh made their way to the gymnasium.

"Lots of guys in the service these days, girls probably don't see as many men around."

The gym was a huge gray stone building, surrounded by sturdy maple trees. Josh pushed open a red metal door and they stepped into a long corridor illuminated by two dim screened-over light bulbs.

"Think I hear some activity down this way," said Cole. He turned down a row of lockers.

At the end of the row a metal door was just swishing shut.

Stenciled on the door were the words: "No One Allowed On Gym Floor Without Proper Shoes.

"I've always been properly attired," said Cole as he opened the door.

"They mean sneakers," said Josh, "but we got no time to run out and buy a couple pairs."

"Odd," murmured Cole. The gym was dark, the bleachers empty. Moonlight coming in through the wired windows made everything look an icy blue.

A door at the other end of the gym floor slammed shut.

Josh put his hand against his companion's arm. "Let's go slow," he said. "I'm starting to get a funny feeling about our door-slamming friend."

Cautiously, watching the shadows which ringed the gym, they began to cross the moonlit wooden floor.

When they were halfway across, a grinding, whirring sound filled the place.

This was the kind of gymnasium that had its swimming pool beneath the floor. The floor opened in the middle and slid aside to give access to the pool below.

The floor was rapidly opening now.

Before Josh and Cole could get clear they both fell through the new opening. They plummeted down toward darkness.

MacMurdie's breath came out in frosty wisps. He rubbed his hands together before continuing on through the bleak woods above the lodge they were seeking. He was alone; the Avenger was approaching the Brotherhood hideout from another angle.

"Whoosh," said Mac to himself, "I do nae take to the bleak weather they have in these parts. I'd much prefer hunting skurlies who are holed up in Florida or California."

The night wind brushed roughly at him, shook the dry branches of the trees.

Another fifty yards and Mac saw the lodge.

"All dark and quiet as a kirkyard at midnight."

The big dark lodge seemed to radiate silence and emptiness.

" 'Twould be a pity were the poor lass's father not here."

They had left Lizbeth Kearny, much against her wishes, back at the Bleek Street headquarters under the watchful eye of Smitty. Nellie was there, too, keeping an eye on both of them. Broome and the other captured members of the Brotherhood of the Millennium were also still at the Justice, Inc. buildings, safely under lock and key. The Avenger didn't want to turn them over to the authorities yet—chiefly because at this point he wasn't certain which authorities he could trust.

Mac worked his way closer to the lodge. He stopped at the edge of the wood, watching the silent place. "I'd take my oath there's no one here."

Very carefully, bent low, the Scot darted out of the cover of the trees. A moment later he was huddled in the shadows beneath the back porch.

Blowing on his hands, rubbing them against each other, MacMurdie said to himself, "I think I'll risk a look inside this little hideaway."

He eased out into the open. His foot was about to hit the lowest step of the back porch stairs when a voice cut through the night, ordering him, "Stop!"

Mac backed, turned to face the Avenger. He patted the top of his head. "Whoosh, you gave me a wee bit of a fright, Richard."

The Avenger was standing ten feet from him,

hands on hips. "They've flown the coop, I'm afraid, Mac."

"Well then, it will no hurt anything if I go inside and nose about some."

"Wait," said the Avenger. He was holding a heavy length of branch in his hand, about three feet long. "Come back here."

Mac gave an obliging shrug and joined Benson.

The Avenger narrowed one eye, flung the log expertly at the back steps of the lodge.

The log thudded down on the top step. A silent second passed. Then the entire porch exploded. The rear door of the lodge blew out with a roar. Flames began jabbing out into the night.

Mac picked himself up off the ground where the concussion had knocked him. He scratched at his sandy head once again. "Appears those skurlies left a booby trap behind for us," he said. "I wonder where they've gotten to."

"I think I know," said the Avenger.

CHAPTER XVII

The Secret of Poseidon

Cole Wilson rose up to the surface of the chill black water and somebody shot at him.

He went back down underwater. "Just like shooting fish in a barrel," he thought to himself. "Except it seems to me I read someplace once that shooting fish in a barrel wasn't all that easy. Let us hope so."

Up very close to the surface there was a faint trace of light. But down here it was completely dark.

Cole frog-kicked down toward the bottom of the pool. He'd dropped in at about the middle of the thing, so the water should be about six feet deep at this point. He stroked his way toward the other end of the pool.

"Maybe if I were Esther Williams I'd get

more of a kick out of this." Cole emerged and took in another breath of air.

A flashlight beam swept across the surface of the pool and caught him. A pistol shot followed.

By that time Cole was underwater again. "Only one of them up there," he decided, "could be kindly old Professor Taverner himself."

Swiftly he swam toward the other end of the indoor pool. He hadn't seen anything of Josh yet.

A moment later his hand brushed against metal. It was the bottom of the ladder which led up out of the shallow end.

Cole caught hold, pulled himself up. His chest was burning and his head felt as though it was about to burst. But he fought off the impulse to surface and suck in air.

He made his way slowly up the ladder. When he was six inches below the surface he saw a hazy glow of light that appeared to be floating up somewhere above him. "The old gent's flashlight," said Cole to himself. "He's taking a shot at Josh. So now's the time to take a little action."

He thrust himself up out of the water, scrambled over the top of the metal ladder. He was weighted down with his soggy clothes. This cut down his speed considerably.

"Ah, there, young man," said Taverner. He was standing on the blue tile which rimmed the pool, .38 revolver in one hand and flashlight in the other.

Cole was on the tiles now. He figured his only chance was to make a head on charge.

But his foot slipped.

That was what saved his life. The rumpled professor had fired at the spot he assumed the charging Cole would be.

Cole wasn't there, though. He was sliding flatout over the wet tiles, like a ballplayer determined to make it to second base ahead of the ball.

His feet hit hard into Taverner's ankle, bowling the older man over.

Taverner's spine cracked against the tile pool edge as he sat suddenly down. He skidded backwards, hands windmilling. Then he toppled over into the dark pool. "Can't swim a stroke," he cried while falling.

"I got him," called Josh from down in the water.

Dripping, Cole moved over to scan the pool. "You okay, Josh?"

"Yeah, he didn't hit me. You?"

"No wounds," answered Cole. "But I'm going to have to stop wearing my good clothes on these jobs."

"Will you gentlemen stop the chitchat and rescue me," spluttered the professor.

The Avenger came striding across his office and sat down behind his desk.

Nellie, her stenographic notebook slapping against her thigh, followed him into the room. "I like your hair that way, Cole," she remarked, sitting down near him.

Cole was in dry clothes now, but his hair was still somewhat damp looking. "Anyone who would wear a snood like the one you had on the other day shouldn't cast stones."

MacMurdie asked the Avenger, "What did the professor have to say?"

"Is my father alive?" asked Lizbeth Kearny.

The Avenger turned his expressionless face toward her. "Yes, he's alive," he said.

"Do you know where he is?"

"They've taken him with them to help locate the Atlantis treasure," said Benson.

"Whereabouts," asked Mac, "is this treasure dig to take place?"

"Taverner told me what he'd learned when he translated that inscription," said Benson. "According to the professor, the message was written by a Phoenician seaman over two thousand years ago. He indicated, this sailor, where he had hidden the treasures he'd salvaged when the continent of Atlantis sank forever into the sea. The place he reached was the island of Decimo."

"That's one of the Azores group," said Josh.

"Yes," said the Avenger. "That's where we'll go. But Josh and Nellie will stay here with the prisoners."

"Going to be tough to get clearance for a trip like that in wartime and all," said the giant Smitty.

"I've already arranged everything," said Benson.

"Thought you didna want to bring the government in on this yet?" said MacMurdie.

"It makes no difference now," answered the Avenger. "I know who the top men are. Taverner gave me the names. So I know who can be trusted and who can't."

"So who's the top dog?" asked Cole.

"We'll see very soon," said Benson. "Now we have to get ready for our jaunt."

"I'm coming along," said Lizbeth. "You can't make me stay here this time."

The Avenger looked at her for several seconds. "Yes, you can come with us," he said finally.

CHAPTER XVIII

The Tenth Island

The Azore Islands are located in the North Atlantic a little over two thousand miles east of New York. They belong to Portugal and were settled by that country in the fifteenth century. Their name derives from the Portuguese name for goshawk. During the age of exploration and discovery the islands were a major stopping place for ships bound for the New World. There is some evidence that they were visited many centuries before the Portuguese came.

The islands which make up the archipelago have a semi-tropical climate and vegetation. There are several supposedly extinct volcanoes in the islands as well as hot springs and what the guide books refer to as other volcanic phenomena. The largest island in the group is São

Miguel. Ten miles north of it lies Decimo, the tenth island.

Decimo has an area of sixty square miles, a population of fifteen thousand people. The chief small industries of the island are sugar refining, tobacco and tea processing, and pineapple growing. There are many fishermen and whalers on the island. The temperature in the late autumn of the year rarely falls below sixty degrees.

On this particular November morning the temperature was sixty-two. A pleasant hazy day. The very fat man at the outdoor table of the little waterfront café was finishing his second cup of coffee with cream and sugar and looking out across the cobblestone street at the calm Atlantic. A crippled old woman in a black shawl went hobbling by, carrying an unwrapped loaf of black bread. A three-legged mongrel dog followed her.

Lund shivered, turned away. That was the trouble with these less-developed parts of the world. They let all sorts of people run around loose. He picked up another slice of buttered sweet bread. "But the food is not too bad," he thought to himself. "Probably a good deal better that it's going to be when I join the others up in the wilderness tomorrow."

Three fishermen, in dark jackets and caps, came climbing up the stone steps of the dock. They all glanced at Lund. Decimo, even back in the peacetime years, never got a great many tourists.

A small boy with a dirty patch over one eye, wearing only a castoff jacket, came up to Lund with his cupped hands held out. "Senhor?"

"You've got my number, haven't you?" said the very fat man. "Got me pegged as a soft touch tourist."

The boy took a step closer.

"Go away," Lund told him.

The boy didn't move.

"I gave you something yesterday, didn't I? Or maybe it wasn't you at that. I can't tell the beggars apart around here."

"Senhor?"

"Okay, okay." Lund dug a few coins out of his coat pocket. "Now let me see which of these are escudos and which are centavos." He poked at the half-dozen coins arrayed on his palm, selected one and flipped it toward the boy.

"*Muito 'brigado,*" he called as he caught it in midair.

After the beggar ran off Lund said to himself, "Probably has a barrel full of money hidden at home. Well, I suppose it's only fair to give them a little something . . . since we're going to be taking several million dollars away from them."

Smiling, he puffed up out of his chair, sorted through the coins again and dropped some on the table top.

The local policeman rode by on his bicycle and gave him a friendly salute.

This made Lund smile even more broadly.

The representatives of law and order he'd seen so far didn't look any too efficient.

"Keystone cops," he said to himself.

Lund walked slowly, his huge body swaying. He puffed, breathing through his mouth as he climbed the cobbled street which led up to the little inn where he was staying. The muggy heat of the morning made him perspire profusely.

A moustached man sitting on the whitewashed stone steps of one of the narrow stone houses was playing a guitar.

At the corner two men in the jackets and trousers of fishermen were standing, listening to the music, laughing and talking, gesturing.

One of them drifted casually across the street as Lund went puffing by. He fell in beside the very fat man.

Lund scowled. "No more handouts today," he said.

"Whoosh, 'tis not a handout I'm after, mon. 'Tis your own sweet self."

Lund stopped dead, blinking. "What's that?"

MacMurdie said, "Would ye be so kind as to step into that alley yonder?" He nudged the very fat man in the side with what felt like a pistol.

"You're not a fisherman."

"No more than you're a tourist," answered Mac. "Now move."

CHAPTER XIX

The Stalking of M1

Cole Wilson put his hands up to the frames of his dark glasses as he grinned at the pretty dark-haired girl who was walking by on the midday street.

"*Muito lindo*," observed the toothless man Cole was in the process of negotiating with.

"That she is," Cole said in his reasonably good Portuguese. "Now about renting your horse and cart."

The toothless man was wearing a blue blazer about two sizes too large and a straw cap which had been fashioned to look like a yachtsman's cap. The Portuguese flag was depicted on the top of the hat. "I notice, senhor, that you are admiring my chapeau. If you'd like a half dozen in assorted sizes as a souvenir of—"

"I'm trying to set a fashion trend away from hats, as a matter of fact," said Cole. "Not that it isn't a handsome piece of headgear. Fifteen escudos for the use of your horse and wagon for the rest of the day."

"Ah, senhor, my services alone are worth that," smiled the toothless man. "Add to that the cost of the horse and this commodious wagon, with its attractive canvas awning to shelter you and your companions from the heat of the sun and—"

"We don't want your services," Cole explained. "We need the cart to take us up into the hills." He took a step away from the man, stood surveying the red and gold wooden cart. There were two rows of red seats inside it and a candy-stripe awning, with red fringe, over it.

"You mean you want to leave me here and make off with the sole source of my livelihood, senhor?"

"How about a deposit of twenty-five escudos?" said Cole. "So if we don't come back you'll have something to tide you over—though I must mention that I'm one of the few good surrey drivers left in America. And I can also handle a sled. Plus twenty escudos for the use of the animal and the handsome wagon."

"Twenty and twenty-five is very near to fifty," pointed out the toothless man. "Let us say fifty and perhaps we have a deal."

"Fifty it is." Cole held out his hand.

The road leveled out and passed between two neat man-high hedges. In the field on their left, far in the distance, was a row of three windmills. On the right, several miles off, rose a flattened-off gray mountain.

"That's the island's extinct volcano over there," said Cole. He was sitting in the front of the rented cart, reins in his hand.

Lizbeth sat next to him and Mac was sitting sideways in the back chairs. Smitty and Benson walked alongside the cart.

"The place we want is supposed to be about a mile this side of that volcano," said the Avenger.

"What's it like up there?" Smitty asked.

"According to the maps I checked over at the police station," said Benson, "it's mostly jungle. There are quite a few rocky hills cropping up out of the vegetation."

"That's where this cavern is supposed to be, huh?"

"Yes, what we learned when we questioned Lund this morning agrees with what Taverner told us as to the location of the hidden treasure."

"And you're certain they have my father with them?" said Lizbeth from the cart.

Benson nodded up at her. "Yes, Lund confirmed that, too."

"I hope he's alright," said the girl.

"They haven't harmed him," the Avenger assured her.

" 'Tis nae likely they will," put in MacMurdie. "He's too valuable to their bullyboy plans."

Cole was making a clucking noise at the piebald horse.

"What's that for?" Lizbeth asked him.

"That's how you talk to horses," he replied,

grinning over at her. "Plus which you use your hands on the reins to communicate. It's rather a fine art."

"I'm fortunate having you along, I guess." She folded her arms, turned to watch the fields.

"I see what your difficulty is," said Cole, making another odd sound in the direction of the horse.

"What difficulty?"

"You're trying to think of a way to apologize to me and you can't come up with the proper one," he said. "Naturally that makes you feel quarrelsome."

"I don't have anything to apologize about."

"See the lengths you're going to to avoid it? But I understand," he said. "I can appreciate the deep chagrin you feel at having to tell me that my notions about how to find your father were much better than yours."

"I admitted that already, didn't I?"

"Grudgingly."

MacMurdie stood up. "Whoosh," he said. "I believe I'll walk beside the cart for a spell. There's too grit an amount of blether going on to suit me." He vaulted over the side.

"How many men can we expect to meet up there?" Smitty asked Benson.

"Four or five according to Lund," he answered. "And one of them will be M1 himself, the top man."

"That's a meeting I'm looking forward to," said Mac.

The Avenger said, "So am I."

CHAPTER XX

The Treasure of Atlantis

Slaw dropped his shovel on the rocky floor of the cavern, straightened up and wiped the back of his hand across his sweating forehead. Late afternoon sunlight knifed into the dark cave, hit the green glass wine bottles near the opening and made them flare an intense emerald color. Slaw walked back and picked up a bottle, uncorked it and took a long pull. "You sure that fool Taverner read those scratches right?"

There were four other men in the cavern. Two others who were engaged in digging. Another man who sat stolidly against the jagged wall with a .32 revolver dangling from his trigger finger. The fourth man was lean, gray-haired, and in his sixties.

This was Norbert A. Kearny. "Taverner is

better than I am at that sort of translating," he said.

"That doesn't mean he's right or accurate," said Slaw. "We've gone the three feet he said. And found nothing yet."

"You must remember you're looking for something which was buried over two thousand years ago," said Kearny. "The earth can change, not perhaps a great deal but some at any rate, in that—"

"I don't need a lecture." Slaw set the wine bottle down with a clink, wiped his mouth and spit out into the hazy afternoon jungle that showed beyond the cave opening.

"I assumed you brought me along for some purpose."

"Had it been my choice to make we would have left you at the lab to work. But you're supposed to be an expert on this Atlantis business, so you were brought."

"The choice was not mine," said Kearny.

After slapping his hands together a few times, Slaw picked up his shovel and resumed digging.

The day faded, darkness came flowing through the thick forest. Slaw was leaning on the handle of his shovel, watching the other two men dig. "Well, Kearny, we're down five feet at the exact spot your damned medallion told us to dig and we sure haven't—"

The tip of one of the other spades hit against metal.

The two diggers stopped, looked across the cavern at Slaw. The man with the gun hanging from his finger grunted.

Slaw grabbed up an oil lantern and, after striking three wax matches, got it lit. He carried it over to the deep hole in the cave floor. "Clear away a little more dirt," he ordered the other two men. "Go easy, don't muck anything up. Come on over here, Kearny."

The professor, prodded by the free hand of the man with the gun, stood up. His legs were stiff from having been sitting in the shadowy cave most of the day.

The light of the lantern seemed to throb, splashing yellow over the men who circled the dark hole. Slowly, cautiously, one of the men was shoveling the dirt off a large, four feet by four feet at least, metal chest.

"Let me handle it now." Slaw hopped into the pit, legs straddling the find. He bent and brushed away the last of the dirt with his hands. There were inscriptions scratched on the heavy lid, and a crude representation of Poseidon's trident. "What do you think, Kearny?"

"Yes, that's what you're seeking."

Slaw climbed out of the hole, nodded at the two other men. "Work on that and get it loose, then get a rope around it so we can haul it out of there." He took a few steps back from the pit. "You don't look very enthusiastic, professor. Considering what a valuable find we've just made."

"Since I've been in the custody of you people," he replied, "I've lost a good deal of my enthusiasm."

"You should be glad we didn't keep up your shots for this trip," said Slaw. "At least you got a clear head to enjoy all this with."

"I'm most appreciative."

There was a faint shuffling sound outside the cave.

The man with the dangling gun sprang to his feet, gun aimed now at the entrance.

Slaw, tugging his own weapon out of his waistband, trotted to the opening. "You're just in time, M1," he said. "We just found it."

Kearny gazed at the darkness with considerable interest. In all the months he'd been a prisoner of the Brotherhood and been forced to work on chemical and biological weapons for them he'd never yet met the man at the top of the organization. And now here was M1 himself about to step into this cavern.

"There's not much time," said Asa Grimshaw as he stepped in out of the murky night.

"Good lord," exclaimed Kearny when he recognized the Secretary of the Navy.

"Good to see you again, Norbert," said Grimshaw. "They've been very anxious about you in Washington."

"You mean . . . you mean you're the top man in this . . . this insane Brotherhood?"

"Insane perhaps," smiled Grimshaw, "but quite efficient."

"I should have realized someone high up in the government was involved," said the professor. "The way so much was known about me, all my top secret work. And even the easy time we had getting here to these islands."

"Yes, of course," answered the white-haired Secretary, "I read all the confidential reports on your project as they came in. The things you were working on seemed ideally suited to our purposes." He walked over to stare down into the pit.

Kearny realized what he was seeing. "You can walk."

"Yes, I was only actually paralyzed for a very short time," answered Grimshaw. "I've found, however, that people don't tend to think a cripple is capable of much, despite some examples in high places. So I stuck to my wheelchair long after I ceased to need it. Easy there."

The two men had the chest up out of its burying place. They swung it over onto solid ground.

"I know of several places where I'll be able to sell these things," said Grimshaw. "It will provide the Brotherhood of the Millennium with more than sufficient funds for the coup we plan." He looked away from the chest, his eyes glowing in the lantern light. "Soon, very soon, Norbert, the rule of the Brotherhood will begin. A rule destined to last at least one thousand years. Great times are coming . . . I offer you the opportunity of working for us of your own free will. Then you will have a very high position when the reign of the Brotherhood begins."

"The only way I'll work for you is against my will," answered the professor.

"Suit yourself." Grimshaw again turned his attention to the metal treasure chest.

Slaw knelt beside it. "Why did you say we had to hurry when you came in?" he asked M1.

"We've had a very slight setback," said Grimshaw.

"Setback?"

"Regrettably the Avenger and some of his crew are on Decimo," answered the Secretary. "They got hold of Lund earlier today."

"Then they'll know where we are," said Slaw. "That fat idiot will tell everything he knows."

"Yes, that's quite likely," said Grimshaw. "Now if you'll open that chest we'll take a look at our treasure."

Kearny, despite what he felt at the moment, found himself highly curious as to what the chest would contain. For years he had read everything he could about the fabled lost continent, he'd dreamed of lost Atlantis, conjectured on what the island colony might have been like.

Slaw had been running his fingers under the rim of the lid. "Doesn't seem to be a lock of any kind. Maybe you're just supposed to lift it." He tried that.

With a raspy creak the lid rose up. Grimshaw snatched the lantern from its resting place on a black rock and held it directly over the chest.

They all looked inside. Even the man with the dangling gun was curious.

Kearny began laughing. "Looks like you're a few hundred years too late, Grimshaw," he said.

The ancient chest was completely empty.

Grimshaw whirled angrily on him. "You knew this all along!"

"Not at all," Kearny said. "I expected a treasure, though I'm not surprised there isn't one. Two thousand and some years is a long time. Obviously somebody else got here first, quite a few centuries ago I'd guess."

"But we have the medallion," insisted Grimshaw, "it's the only key to the location."

"Perhaps our long dead Phoenician made more than one medallion," suggested Kearny. "Or perhaps the men who found the treasure of Atlantis later lost the medallion."

"Where's the treasure then?"

"By now it may be scattered to the ends of the earth."

The secretary scowled at the empty chest, then at the men standing around him. "All of you," he ordered, "dig some more. There may be something else down there, there has to be."

"We went deeper than—" began Slaw.

"Get to digging," shouted Grimshaw. "Do as I tell you."

Slaw said, "But you told us we haven't much time."

"You haven't any time," said a level voice from the mouth of the cave.

"The Avenger!" said Grimshaw.

146

Richard Henry Benson stood there, just touched by the lantern light. His odd and highly individual gun was in his hand. "I'm afraid the Brotherhood isn't going to have its thousand year reign," he told them.

CHAPTER XXI

Tremor

Slaw kicked the lantern, suddenly, into the pit. The glass smashed, the light sputtered out and there was only blackness in the cavern.

At least two guns spoke now, both firing at the cave entrance where the Avenger had been standing.

Then there was silence. Out in the jungle a few night birds called, insects chirped.

"Did you get him?" asked Grimshaw in a rasping whisper.

"I think so," said Slaw.

"Find out."

Slaw pressed his back to the rocky wall, began inching his way sideways toward the jagged opening of the cave.

Before he reached the exit something hit the

cavern floor and smashed. Something small and made of glass.

"Watch out," warned Slaw. "It's some kind of gas I think—"

A second pellet was tossed in from somewhere outside to smash on the rocks.

"Stop them," yelled Grimshaw. "Shoot them down."

Slaw couldn't reply because he was coughing now, harsh hacking coughs that sent needles ripping through his lungs. Tears were spouting out of his eyes, zigzagging down his cheeks. He tried to fire a shot out there at whoever had done this to him. He sneezed instead.

The man who'd dangled his gun gave in first. He had been coughing and crying, bent half over, gagging and trying to gasp in air. Shaking his head in desperation, he ran out into the night and threw his weapon away from him. "There goes my gun," he cried out. "Help me now, do something to stop this."

Giant hands plucked him off the ground and carried him in among a stand of palm trees. Something with a bitter smell was held under his running nose. In a few seconds the pains in his chest and head subsided. He tried to wipe his nose and then realized his hands were tied behind his back. The big man who'd grabbed him dropped him to the mossy ground.

"How many more inside there?" Smitty asked him.

The man gave one more sneeze before answering. "I don't know . . . let me see. Slaw and

the old guy and the professor . . . and Gores
and . . . I forget his name but his number is
M10034."

"Mon," said Mac, who was standing nearby,
"in the time he's rattled them off most of them
skurlies and Kearny have come tumbling out."

Cole and the Avenger, who had thrown himself out of range the instant the lantern went
sailing for the pit, were disarming the dazed
Brotherhood agents as they came, wobbling and
staggering, out of the treasure cave.

Lizbeth Kearny ran across the swarm and
threw her arms around her father. "Dad, are
you alright?"

The old man was crying, sneezing and coughing. He made several yawning faces, trying to
focus on the girl. "Liz . . . Liz, how did you get
here?"

"With the Avenger, with the people from
Justice, Inc."

MacMurdie ran over to them and broke a
small phial under the professor's nose. "You'll
feel like a newbairn babe shortly," he promised.

"Yes, I seem to be coming out of it," said
Kearny. "That's very interesting stuff you have
there. What exactly are the—?"

"Father," said his redhaired daughter. "You
can talk shop later."

The professor could see her now. He put his
hands on her slim shoulders, took a step back.
Smiling, he said, "There were a great many
times when I thought I'd never be this close to
you again, Liz."

"I know . . . and for a while I thought . . . I got the awful idea you might be . . . I don't know, in cahoots with these people, with the Brotherhood of the Millennium."

"Yes, I suppose after all those months," her father said, "you'd be ready to believe most anything, Liz. But I can assure you I worked for them only when they . . . well, when they made it impossible for me not to."

"You did send me a message, though."

The professor laughed. "Yes, I overheard enough of their conversations to know that my desperate scheme with poor Glanz had worked."

"That's why we're here," said Lizbeth. "Though it was a roundabout sort of thing."

"They moved me from place to place a lot," said Kearny. "Ever since that morning when they grabbed me on my way to talk to Taverner. I let my hobby really get the best of me that time."

Cole, with the help of Smitty and Mac, had all the men except Grimshaw tied securely.

The Avenger himself was standing with his gun covering the leader of the Brotherhood. "By now the rest of your men, at least the top echelon, have been picked up," said Benson. "I cabled Washington and New York once I knew for sure you were here."

"Very sure of yourself, Richard Henry," said the white-haired man, "as usual."

"An idea like yours, Asa, could never have—"

The earth all around them began to shake. The trees rattled violently as though visited by

151

a huge wind. A mile across the night, red fire began to spit up into the dark sky.

"Whoosh, 'tis the volcano going off," cried Mac.

Another vicious tremor snapped the ground and caused the Avenger to stumble sideways.

Grimshaw kicked out. His heavy boot connected with Benson's temple.

The Avenger dropped to his knees.

Grimshaw ran.

"No, you don't," said Smitty. He took off after the running man.

The Secretary ran well and fast. He made it into the jungle beyond the cave before Smitty had even gotten past the fallen Benson.

The ground was hopping madly, the whole jungle seemed about to tumble down. Red streaks were gashing across the dark, millions of sparks flickered and died and were reborn. A roar filled the air. It was as though some great wild beast were imprisoned beneath the earth and trying to rend free.

Grimshaw came to a clearing in the woods, a wide stretch of mossy ground with a small pool in its center. The black water of the pool was splashing and spilling, frothing.

Smitty sprinted, cutting down the distance between him and the other man. "You haven't got a chance of—"

Smitty saw what was happening and pulled himself to a stop.

The ground was shaking and shaking ever more violently. With an echoing brittle sound it suddenly ripped open. A wide jagged crack went cutting across yards and yards of the clearing.

Grimshaw had no chance to escape. His right foot had been in midair when the vast crack shot by under him. He stepped down into nothing. Fell into the earth, crying out.

The jungle vibrated, branches snapped from the trees, cascades of leaves came flapping down. The crack closed up. Grimshaw was gone.

Smitty stood there. Slowly he reached up one big hand and brushed away the bits of palm frond and leaves which had settled on his head and shoulders.

He turned and made his way back through the jungle. There were a few more tremors, not strong.

"For an extinct volcano," Cole was saying when Smitty got back near the cave, "that's a pretty good imitation of a live one."

The Avenger was on his feet, MacMurdie beside him, looking as though nothing had happened. "Where's Grimshaw?" he asked the returning Smitty.

Smitty stroked his chin. "Well," he said, "you're maybe not going to believe this . . . but the ground swallowed him up." He told them what he'd witnessed back there in the clearing.

The night sky still seemed to be burning, but the earth had ceased shaking and trembling.

"We're finished here," Benson said.

Professor Kearny coughed. "If we could I'd like to bring that empty chest home with us," he said. "I'm not sure of it's authenticity yet, but it's the closest I'm likely to come to the treasure of Atlantis."

CHAPTER XXII

Round Up

MacMurdie was behind the soda fountain in his drugstore, polishing soft-drink glasses. The first edition of the evening paper was spread out on the counter so that he could read it while he worked. "Whoosh," he said, "would ye look at that. They've rounded up nearly nine hundred of them Brotherhood skurlies already."

The giant Smitty, hands locked behind his back, was standing in front of the newsstand. "More and more comic books coming out every month," he said. "I think they're going to catch on." He came over and sat on one of the counter stools. "I notice they didn't give Justice, Inc. any credit."

"That's the way Dick wanted it," said Mac as he held a glass up to the overhead light.

"I got the notion he's expecting a visitor tonight," said Smitty. "By the way he kind of hinted we could all take some time off."

After giving the glass one more vigorous wipe, Mac set it aside. "Aye, I believe 'tis one of them hush-hush government laddies come down to talk with him."

"Don't tell me they're still mad because we stuck our nose in the man from Atlantis business?"

"I don't know whether they've come to chastise him or to pin a medal on him," said MacMurdie. "But if I know Dick he won't tell us what happened, whichever it is."

Cole Wilson rotated the swizzle stick once in his drink and grinned across the candlelit table. "I knew you'd come to your senses sooner or later."

Lizbeth Kearny said, "I am grateful to you, Cole. The least I can do is have dinner with you before I go away."

Dropping the swizzle stick on the crisp white table cloth, Cole asked, "You're going away, angel?"

"My father and I are, yes."

"Where to?"

"I can't tell you exactly," said the redhaired girl. "Out west someplace, though. My father decided, after what the Brotherhood of the Millennium had in mind for his proposed weapons, that he didn't want to work on them any longer."

"A good idea, though it probably won't keep that stuff from coming into being."

"No, but at least my father will be able to feel that he had nothing directly to do with the weapons," said the girl. "Nowadays . . . well, it's difficult to know to what uses you should put your knowledge. There are so many terrible things that . . ." She let the sentence trail off, then attempted a smile. "Very gloomy conversation for my going away dinner."

"You've put me in a gloomy mood," said Cole. "A blighted romance always does."

"I think you'll bounce back."

"Certainly I'll bounce back," said Cole. "That's the worst part of it."

The clean-cut young man with the tan overcoat over his arm sat down opposite Dick Benson's big desk. "This isn't an official visit," he said.

"I realize that," said the Avenger. "Officially you and your agency don't even exist."

Don Early smiled. "I just wanted you to know that we appreciate what you and Justice, Inc. did," he said. "Even though we would have preferred you keep away from the whole business."

"Did you have any idea Secretary Grimshaw was involved in the abduction of Professor Kearny?"

"No," admitted Early. "In fact, a word he put to our agency to keep this thing quiet was one of the reasons for my leaning on you the way I did."

Benson leaned back in his chair, brought the tips of his fingers together against his chin. No emotion showed on his face, but there was an intense glow illuminating his eyes. "The kind of weapons Kearny was working on shouldn't be used by anyone," he said. "I knew something about what he'd been working on for you. That's why it was important to find him."

"Don't get the idea he was working on orders from me," said the clean-cut Early. "I only work for the government, I don't make the policies."

"That's one reason why there's a Justice, Inc.," said Benson. "We don't have to worry about anybody's policies but our own."

Early shifted, a little uncomfortably, in his chair. He cleared his throat, then stood up. "Well, I wanted to thank you for what you did," he said. "I'll be running along. Perhaps we'll run into each other again."

"Perhaps." Benson showed the young man out of his office.

The Avenger returned to his desk and sat down again. He put the tips of his fingers together against his chin once more.